EXECUTIVE BEDTIME STORIES

Soothing Tales for Stressful Times

by A. L. Jagoe

Quill & Penny Publishing
Kensington, MD.

© 1993 Quill & Penny Publishing, Kensington, Maryland.

All rights reserved. No part of this work covered by the copyright hereon may be reproduced or used in any form or by any means—graphic, electronic, or mechanical, including photocopying, recording, taping, or information storage and retrieval systems—without written permission of the publisher.

ISBN 0-9636561-0-4
Printed and bound in the United States of America

Illustrations by Kathryn L. Williams

Dedication

To five grandkids,

Emma

Georgina

Karim

Ricky

Royston

Acknowledgments

I want to express my appreciation to the many friends whose ideas and suggestions have been of value in the writing of this book. Among them are Dick Andrews, Fred Bellamah, Wright Poffenberger, Sommers Brown, Malcolm Bund, David Dawson, Nick Kronfeld, DeMar Keller, Burns McLindon, Carlos Rodriguez and Dick Stout.

Paul Cummins, Bob Gray, Hal Schwartz, and Joel Tumarkin were invaluable as my "kitchen advisors."

Special bouquets go to my editorial critics, Sandy Trupp and Eva Jagoe, who contributed countless hours of solid advice.

The top accolade goes to my editor, Phil Trupp. He is an outstanding teacher, sparring partner, and friend. Phil has the rare trait of being a perfectionist with a great sense of humor.

Table of Contents

	An Introduction: Required Reading *ix*
1.	My Son, the Emma-B-A *1*
2.	Just Like the Big Boys *7*
3.	Ambrose *14*
4.	Biz-Scent *19*
5.	High-Level Assignment *26*
6.	Gotcharonovinski *35*
7.	How to Pick a Winning Stock *42*
8.	Dealer's Tale *48*
9.	Deficit Reduction, Homestyle *56*
10.	T. E., Inc. *61*
10-A.	Tennis Reinvented *68*
12.	Skirmish of the Sexes *75*
13.	Drexel Fallout *82*
14.	It Was a Very Good Year—Almost *87*
15.	Marx Brothers *93*
16.	Personal Service *102*
17.	A Tooth Grows in Brooklyn *107*
18.	Questionable Light Bill *112*
19.	Billy Goat Syndrome *117*
20.	School for Executives *123*
21.	Assolds *132*

22. Boomerang *137*
23. Executive Toys *143*
24. Sinful Businessman *150*
25. Postman's Wife *155*
26. Fini La Vacation *162*
27. Wynmill Dichotomy *167*
28. Tale of Wall Street *174*
29. Salary Adjustment, at Your Own Expense *180*
30. Paul's Tale *186*
31. Yellow Butterfly and Pigeon with Pink Toes *192*

Introduction

The purpose of *Executive Bedtime Stories* is to use a light touch in helping the business and professional world look at itself. I am convinced that if we can view our problems and concerns with a relaxed sense of awareness, solutions will follow.

This collection of stories, many of which are based on actual experiences, was sparked by a call from a friend. He asked for a copy of a satire I had written some years ago about the insurance industry, where I have spent a large part of my professional life. He had misplaced his copy which he kept handy in his top desk drawer.

"Whenever I get depressed," he said, "I reread your article. It always gives me a lift."

I asked if he recalled the many educational articles I had published in the meantime. After a long pause, he admitted remembering only the one that made him laugh.

I found the same was true of my book, *The Winning Corporation*. Everyone remembered the story I told about my friend, the late Petie Green, an ex-con with a sixth-grade education. When being refused federal funding because his organization's creed had used the word "God," Petie said to the government official, "Okay, Buster, you take it off the dollar bill, and I'll take it off my creed."

One word of advice: Each story has its own distinct message. I recommend reading only one a night. To do otherwise is to risk an overdose.

Executive Bedtime Stories aims to soothe a tired mind, not introduce discord. Therefore, the book does not have a Chapter Eleven.

A. L. Jagoe

Kensington, Maryland

 # 1 My Son, The Emma-B-A

When Henry Thompson walked by the fruit market, Tony, the proprietor, rushed out to greet him.

"Guessa what," Tony said. "My son Gino home from school. He now Emma-B-A."

"Hey, that's great," Henry said. "You must be mighty proud."

A tall young man with thick glasses came out of the store to shake hands.

"Gino, you meet my friend," Tony said proudly.

In the eight years that Henry had practiced law in Gulfport, he didn't recall having met this member of Tony's large family.

"Gino," Henry said, "I've heard so much about you from your father. He told me you stayed on at Harvard for your graduate studies."

Reaching up to put his arm around his son's shoulder, Tony said with a broad grin, "Now Gino Emma-B-A." He gave the young man a hug that pulled him to one side. "Just think," Tony went on,

A. L. Jagoe

"Why I need 'muddled' management?"

"I starta business with nothing. Now I poppa of Emma-B.A."

"Congratulations, Gino," Henry said. "That's quite an accomplishment."

Tony suddenly turned and rushed into the market. He scurried past the lemons and oranges to a white cabinet under two large clusters of bananas. He returned with an expensive red portfolio.

"Look," Tony exclaimed, "you see what Gino do for me."

"In the week that I have been home," Gino

explained, "I did a strategic plan for Poppa's business. I am afraid that it is long overdue."

Tony held the report close to his chest. "But I no understand," he said. "For exam, why I need muddled management?"

"No, Poppa," Gino corrected him. "I said that you need a layer of *middle* management."

Henry asked how that would work.

"You see," Gino explained, "including the wholesale operations, Poppa has over thirty employees he has to supervise one-on-one. Therefore, there is definitely a requirement for another strata of management between Poppa and his employees."

"Why I need?" Tony protested. "I tella what to do. They do. Everybody happy."

Gino smiled kindly at his father then turned to Henry.

"Another problem," he said, "is that Poppa cannot seem to grasp the importance of gaining a tighter control on cash flow."

Before Henry could respond, Tony made a very positive comment. "For thirty-five years," he said, "cash she flow good to educate six kids and take care Momma and me."

Ignoring this remark, Gino explained that he was very familiar with the fruit business. "Two years ago," he said, "I had an article published about the inherent dangers in the produce business. The piece was very well received."

"So you have had experience in this area," Henry said.

Gino thought a moment. "Not exactly what you might call a hands-on confrontation," he replied. "But I researched my study through extensive reading and interviews with some of the larger produce merchants."

"My Gino smart boy," Tony observed with a big grin.

Gino accepted this comment as though it were a confirmation of the obvious.

"Another facet of Poppa's business that disturbs me," Gino said, "is the fact that all operations are centered around one function—the sale of fruit."

Henry agreed that was true.

"But I think Poppa should diversify into other operations that would produce synergistic action with a positive effect on the whole."

"Just what do you have in mind?" Henry asked.

Before answering, the young scholar took several deep breaths. For the purpose of demonstration, he reached down and picked up a large pineapple displayed on the front table. "You do agree with me that fruit is food, right?" Henry nodded. "And you must admit that the more people eat, the better the fruit business. Do you not agree?"

"I guess so."

With a smile of one who has proved his point, Gino concluded with this statement: "Therefore, I think Poppa should invest in a restaurant."

Realizing that he was being stared down by the recent graduate of a prestigious university of higher education, Henry hesitated.

"But, don't you think it would be hazardous for your father to go into a business he's not familiar with? I understand that running a restaurant can be very demanding and risky."

With his head slightly tilted upward, Gino informed him that the principles of good management are the same whether you are running a manufacturing plant, a service business, or a fruit market.

Henry cautiously offered one more comment. "Your father has been very successful in real estate. You probably know that through the years he has amassed considerable commercial property that has increased tenfold in value."

"Yes," Gino replied flatly. "But the ownership of property is not relevant to the fruit business, which has been his chief source of income."

Tony jumped back into the conversation. "I try to make Gino come run business, but he say no."

"Next month," Gino said, "I will begin a position on the university academic staff. I will be teaching a course in strategic planning and marketing."

Still embracing the red portfolio, Tony exclaimed, "I show to all customers." He gave Gino a respectful nudge and said with a smile, "My son, the Emma-B-A."

Just then the telephone rang at the back of the store, and Tony went to answer it.

"Poor Poppa," Gino sighed. "I just cannot seem to get through to him."

"I understand," Henry said. "But maybe it's best

to leave him in his ignorance."

"I suppose you are right," the young man said with resignation. "But poor Poppa."

Moral:

Education plus experience equals success.
Education minus experience equals education.

2 | Just Like The Big Boys

"I have called this special meeting," began the elder Walter Grumpeau in an austere tone, "because I am concerned about the new president of our company." Leaning back in his sturdy leather chair, he looked solemnly across the massive boardroom table at the other two directors.

"I knew it was a mistake," said his younger brother, Willie Grumpeau. "First time we ever had a non-family member as top dog."

"Oh dear," exclaimed sister Matilda Grumpeau, twisting her handkerchief. "I do hope nothing is wrong."

"I am afraid something is terribly wrong," Walter Grumpeau replied, taking a sheet of paper from his pocket. "I have made a list of my concerns. First of all, this young whipper-snapper gave himself a ten percent raise even though profits last year were down."

"Outrageous!" exclaimed Willie.

"Second, there is a mysterious thirty-four thousand dollar item for public relations."

"Perhaps," suggested Matilda, "this might be for advertising or some type of employee benefit."

"Horse feathers!" Willie shot back. "When I was president, we never advertised. As for employees, we give them only what we have to."

"Third," the ancient Grumpeau continued, "I have serious doubts about his projected profits. They seem to be unrealistically inflated."

"I noticed that, too," Willie said.

"It's always good to be optimistic," Matilda offered in a chipper voice.

"There is something else I intend to question," the chairman said. "When we hired him a year ago, I told him I wanted better financial reports, so I authorized him to hire a new controller. This he has not done."

"He probably doesn't want to have a good financial man looking over his shoulder," Willie commented.

Stretching his back, the old gentleman said, "As son of the founder of the company and chairman of this board, I have asked you to be present when I confront our president, Roger Dodger, with these serious matters."

"I'm looking forward to it," said Willie. "I mean, as a member of the board, I consider it my obligation."

Matilda looked as if she would much rather be working with her prize roses or playing bridge. She twisted uneasily in her seat. "Oh me," she sighed, "I don't like confrontations."

"This won't take long," Willie told her. "I intend to be out of here in time for golf at two. I'll give you a ride home."

Walter Grumpeau frowned. "Regardless of the time it will require, we must face up to our responsibility." He pressed the buzzer and said in a hushed tone, "I expect us to present a united front."

Roger Dodger bounded enthusiastically into the room. He was a wiry young man with an expression that looked as if he viewed everything with awe. "My!" he exclaimed. "What a treat to meet again with all the family. How is everyone?"

Silence. Walter Grumpeau and Willie looked at him sternly as if he were an accused criminal standing before the bench. Matilda squirmed as if she were the guilty party.

"Have a seat, Mr. Dodger," the Chairman growled. "There are some serious matters we would like to discuss."

"Gladly," said Roger. He sat down with both elbows on the table. "Fire away."

Referring to his notes, Walter Grumpeau cleared his throat loudly. "I see here," he began, "that you gave yourself a salary increase even though there was a drop in profits."

"That's right," the president agreed.

"And there is a new expense item of thirty-four thousand dollars that I do not understand."

"I know just what you're referring to," he replied.

"Also," the chairman continued, "based on past performance, your future projections seem exaggerated. Perhaps," he added with a tone of sarcasm. "If you had hired a competent controller, I would have more faith in these figures."

The president grinned broadly. "I'm delighted to have the opportunity to discuss these matters with you and to put your minds at ease. But first I want to thank you for the good advice you gave me at our initial meeting. I've tried to follow it faithfully."

The family members looked quizzically at one another. Then Walter Grumpeau asked, "And what advice was that?"

"Remember you said you wanted me to think big and to run this company as if it were one of the *Fortune* 500s. You also gave me authority to hire anyone I wanted as controller."

"Yes, I recall that clearly," Walter Grumpeau agreed. "So why did you not act on this suggestion?"

"I did !" the young president said. "I gave it a lot of thought, and there was only one person I wanted for this job."

"Who was that?" Willie asked.

"Donald Trump."

The chairman sputtered, "Why, that's preposterous!"

Roger reflected for a moment. "Funny thing— that's just what his secretary said when I told her why I was calling."

Willie thumped his fingers on the table. "What about the salary raise?"

"I read a study done by a compensation specialist who reviewed several hundred of the nation's largest corporations. He found little correlation between what a company earns and the amount of executive pay. For example, I read that the two fellows who head Time Warner, Inc., were paid a total of nearly $100 million. The specialist said, based on the performance of the company, they should have received only $3 million."

"Disgusting," muttered Walter Grumpeau.

"Yes," Roger agreed. "And I also read where the head of General Dynamics got a million-six bonus, just because the stock went up ten dollars. And he doesn't have to give it back if the stock drops."

Matilda made several "tut, tut" noises.

"So you see," he continued, "compensation for an American executive is a case of heads you win, tails you win. If I'd followed the example of the executives included in that survey, I would have taken a thirty-two percent increase. Out of modesty, I only took ten percent."

"Bully for you!" Matilda exclaimed. The other two board members glared at her.

The chairman reshuffled his notes. "And this thirty-four-thousand-dollar item for public relations—what can you tell us about that?"

"Oh, that was bribery," the president explained.

Matilda gasped, and put her hand to her mouth.

"You see," the young man continued, "this company has never been successful in its bid for the state maintenance contract. So, I did just like the super executives I read about. For example, with Hughes Aircraft, a vice president bribed to win a multimillion dollar contract. They also were charged with falsifying test results on electronic circuits. UNISYS greased the skids to land a fat award. And General Electric was socked $30 million for fraudulent government billings. So, I slipped a few dollars here and there to get inside information about the contract specifications. And," he said with a satisfied smile, "you're the first to know we won the award. This will double our volume and estimated profits for the year."

Stunned silence filled the room. Walter Grumpeau seemed to be fumbling for something to say. He removed his glasses and wiped them slowly.

The president went on, "And just like General Dynamics, United Technologies, National Health Laboratories, and many other big boys who have been accused of defrauding the government, I intend to overcharge every item we bill. The only problem we'll face a year from now will be taxes on our earnings. And, in anticipation of this record profit," he said, "I've taken the liberty of preparing for each of you a bonus of twenty-five thousand dollars. I hope you'll approve this action after I leave the room." He handed out three checks.

Walter Grumpeau suddenly recovered his voice. "Mr. Dodger, on behalf of the board, I want to commend you for your fine performance."

Carefully folding his check and tucking it in his wallet, Willie said, "Job well done!"

Hesitatingly, Matilda asked, "But is it honest?"

"My dear sister," Walter Grumpeau said, "we are

running a business, not a charity."

Moral:

*Like a chameleon,
corporate values can change color
when sitting on a pile of greenbacks.*

 3 Ambrose

There was a certain mystery about Jeremiah Martindale's office, a mystery as intriguing as the man himself. Near the entrance stood a large saltwater aquarium. An abundance of plants, with palms touching the ceiling, bordered a wall-sized picture window. Occasionally, fellow executives referred to the president's office as "Jeremiah's jungle."

Perhaps the most bizarre touch was an ornate bird cage behind the desk. Inside the cage lived a multicolored parrot, which many years ago had been given to Jeremiah Martindale's mother by a South American missionary. The bird's name was Ambrose.

As one of her morning secretarial chores, Ms. Lane would change the paper in the bottom of Ambrose's cage and give him fresh water, fruit, and seeds. Later, when Jeremiah Martindale arrived, his first act was to confirm that Ambrose had been properly serviced. He alone appreciated the bird's importance to the corporation.

In the presence of others, Ambrose misbehaved only once—it was while a *Wall Street Journal* reporter was interviewing Jeremiah Martindale about the secret of his superb judgement.

The reporter said, "Your people tell me you take a long time to make decisions, but they say it's worth the wait because you're always right."

"Well," Jeremiah Martindale replied, "I credit this ability to my many years of study and experience."

Ambrose let out such a raucous laugh that the reporter nearly bolted out of his seat.

Jeremiah Martindale's style was a bit peculiar. For example, he insisted that all discussions be held in his private office. Another quirk was that, when a meeting ended, he would promise a decision in the near future, but first he needed his "quiet time."

Following a typical meeting in his office, Jeremiah Martindale would carefully lock the soundproof door. He would then go to the bird cage and stare into the parrot's deep black eyes.

"So, Ambrose," he would say quietly. "What do you think?"

The bird would cock his head to one side, stare at his master with half-closed eyes, ruffle his feathers, then squawk a response. The answer was always brief and to the point: "Go with it!" "No way!" "More cash! More cash!" "Go slow, Joe!"

Jeremiah Martindale had discovered Ambrose's remarkable insight many years ago. It happened one day after a lengthy meeting in his office with a

A. L. Jagoe   15

senior vice president who had come up with a corporate restructuring plan.

"Ambrose," he said, "it's a can of worms. What do you think?"

"Fire the bum!" Ambrose squawked.

Jeremiah Martindale was stunned. "But," he protested, "he's one of my top people."

Jeremiah needed his quiet time.

Ambrose squatted several times like a fat man testing the seat of his pants. "Fire the bum!" he screeched. "Fire the bum!"

To the surprise of his executive staff, the following morning Jeremiah Martindale dismissed the vice president. Six weeks later, an internal audit proved that the man had embezzled large sums of money. From that moment on, the Martindale wisdom became legendary.

Under his expert guidance, the company prospered. In annual summaries of American corporations, it constantly received top honors. Revenues doubled every three years, due partly to successful acquisitions. On Wall Street, the company stock was touted by every investment guru.

But Ambrose was not always cooperative. On more than one occasion, he would refuse to answer. When this occurred, Jeremiah Martindale would rub the bird's head. Then he would take off his glasses and hold a sunflower seed in his teeth. Pressing his face against the cage, he would let Ambrose take the seed with his hooked beak.

If none of these tactics worked, he would cover the cage with the night blanket and go home. The next morning, he would anxiously uncover the bird.

"Ambrose," he would say, "you are a naughty little fellow. Now that you've had a good night's sleep, you will get an extra portion of food if you tell me what to do."

With indifference, the bird would give his feathers a good shaking. He would stretch by hanging upside down and swing back and forth. Finally, he would give his master the needed words of advice.

Then one day when Jeremiah Martindale was at his peak of prominence, he stunned the business world by resigning without notice. Even Ms. Lane was taken by surprise. The Board of Directors held a special meeting to try to dissuade the famous president. They were unsuccessful.

The next morning, Ms. Lane lamented to another secretary, "Bad news seems to come in pairs. Yesterday when Mr. Martindale called me into his office to tell me he was quitting, you could have knocked me over with a feather." She sighed and continued, "And earlier that morning, when I went in to take care of Ambrose, I found the little fellow dead in the bottom of his cage."

Moral:
Birds of a feather fly the coop together.

 # 4 Biz-Scent

Horace could tell by the twitching of the prospect's neatly clipped moustache that he was on the verge of a big sale, so he quit talking and sat back.

It was the first time since becoming a salesman for Biz-Scent three months ago that he had been successful in getting to the inner sanctum of a prestigious company. The president's office was like a Fifth Avenue apartment. The floor was covered with a large oriental rug. There was a crystal chandelier, and the massive desk blended in with the other antiques.

From behind the desk inversely proportioned to his small stature, the president, Jacque Bonaparte, said, "Young man, this is an astounding concept. Let me see if I grasp the quintessence of the matter before us. You are telling me that your firm, Biz-Scent, has identified over 3,000 scents, each of which produces a distinct emotional reaction."

"That's right," Horace replied. "With music piped into every office at Bonaparte Industries, you appeal to your employees's sense of hearing. But," he said dramatically, "you overlook the most powerful of all senses—the ability to react to a smell. Biologically speaking, when a fragrance reaches the receptor cells in the nasal cavity behind the bridge of the nose, it's recorded in the olfactory bulb of the brain. This immediately detonates an emotional response."

Just as his sales manual instructed, Horace silently counted to ten before he spoke again.

"Through our extensive research, we have identified the reaction conjured up by each scent. For example, the aroma of spiced apples reduces blood pressure. Jasmine produces a feeling of compassion. Pine inspires neatness, and the list goes on."

The president then asked the question the salesman had been waiting for. Leaning back in his large red leather wing-back chair that looked as if had been designed for a king, he asked, "But how does this apply to Bonaparte Industries?"

"Very simply," Horace replied confidently. "Beginning fifteen minutes before your employees report to work, our computerized system will deposit lavender in the air conditioning system. Lavender is a stimulant aroma that makes one bright and alert. At your ten o'clock coffee break, we'll add mint. This eliminates the mid-morning slump that is costing you many dollars in underproduction. Then at a quarter to twelve, the pot roast aroma will speed up work in anticipation of lunch."

"Amazing!" Mr. Bonaparte exclaimed.

"And our scientific programming of motivating

scents continues until a half-hour before quitting time. As you are aware, this is a sluggish period. But," he said, raising his index finger, "we have the solution. We inject a musty scent that smells like money. This subconsciously induces each employee to strive harder until the last minute of the working day."

"But wouldn't I be manipulating my employees?"

"Of course," Horace answered. "Are you paying your people to come and enjoy themselves at a recreational center? Of course, not!" Then lowering his voice, he added, "Manipulate is too harsh a word. But you agree that if you don't milk as much effort from your employees as you can, you won't have a profit at the end of the year."

Mr. Bonaparte nodded. "It's refreshing," he said. "to hear such wisdom from one who appears to be so young."

Horace smiled. "Why don't I give you a free demonstration."

"How would you do that?" Mr. Bonaparte asked.

The salesman thought for a moment. "Well," he said slowly, "who's your next appointment?"

The president checked his schedule and said, "Simon Turnscrew, my vice president in charge of warehousing."

Horace opened up his large case of samples and studied the labels. He took out two vials and held them up. "By careful blending of scents," he explained, "you can produce certain psychological effects. For example, the aroma that results from mixing one portion of rose oil with two parts of wild boar musk causes a feeling of remorse."

"You don't say."

Horace nodded and continued, "I'll sprinkle it around your office, and we'll see how it works on your next visitor."

Mr. Bonaparte seemed skeptical. "What effect will it have on me?"

"None," he assured him. "You are aware of the test, so you won't have any reaction."

The president gave a nod. Horace quickly sprinkled the mixture on the carpet between the doorway and the desk. Mr. Bonaparte then suggested that Horace hide in the adjacent executive bathroom. He was to remain there quietly with the door closed.

Inside this elaborate room with its gold fixtures, the young salesman was too nervous to sit down. He stood with his ear glued to the door. Unfortunately, all he could hear were muffled voices. In less than ten minutes, Mr. Bonaparte opened the door. His eyes were alive with excitement.

"You won't believe what happened," he sputtered. "A few minutes after Turnscrew began his report, this man who has been my trusted vice president for nine years suddenly took a deep breath and confessed he's been stealing over ten thousand dollars a month through fake invoices. And not only that," he said, "but he gave me the names of other employees who are in on his scam."

Mr. Bonaparte grabbed Horace by the arm and

pulled him down as if he were going to kiss him. Instead, he pinched his cheek. With glee, he announced, "Young man, you have a contract!"

Horace's face lit up. His name could head the top producer list for the month. He ball-parked what his commission would be.

Returning to the security of his desk, Mr. Bonaparte buzzed for his secretary. "Ms. Wellington, please come in to take a letter."

The attractive secretary came in with her note pad. After introducing her to Horace, Mr. Bonaparte asked both to sit while he gave a letter of acceptance to the Biz-Scent Company. Ms. Wellington sat next to the desk, and Horace took a chair in front.

It was difficult for Horace to appear casual. He was afraid they might hear his pounding heart.

After taking a few sentences of dictation, Ms. Wellington suddenly relaxed and put down her pen. She was breathing deeply with her eyes closed. Mr. Bonaparte became alarmed.

"Ms. Wellington," he said, "is anything the matter?"

She made no response. Both men were watching her with concern.

Suddenly she opened her eyes, and looked across at the president. In a voice choked with emotion, she cried, "Jack, we must tell your wife about us."

Mr. Bonaparte's face flushed, and he slumped back into his throne-chair. His facial expression froze in a sick grin. Then he slowly began making a gurgling noise.

As if he were a trained medic, Horace swung into action. From his sample case, he took the scent of spiced apples and waved it in front of the president's face. It worked like magic. In a few seconds, Mr. Bonaparte regained his executive decorum.

Taking the initialed handkerchief from his lapel pocket, he wiped his mouth. Then with the dignity of an archbishop, he said, "Tillie...I mean, Ms. Wellington...that will be all. Thank you."

When the men were alone, Mr. Bonaparte swung his chair to one side and stared at the wall tapestry as if he had never seen it before. "Upon reflection," he said with solemnity, "I often discover that the vicissitudes of the eclectic factors of management require more than a modicum of polemics."

Horace's eyes crossed.

The president continued, "Your service may have value to some indigenous establishments, but I fear that at Bonaparte Industries, it would have an exacerbating effect. Therefore," he concluded, "with great reluctance, I will not avail myself of your services."

Recalling the last chapter in his sales manual, Horace tried to be gracious. "I want to thank you, Mr. Bonaparte," he said, with a frog in his throat, "for the opportunity to demonstrate the advantage of Biz-Scent to your organization." The president continued to stare at the tapestry and strummed his fingers on the desk.

"As a small means of appreciation for your consideration," Horace went on, "I would like to give you a sample of our special scent #1055."

The young salesman quietly left the gift on the desk and walked out of the room.

While sitting in his car in the visitor's parking space, Horace recorded the details of this appointment. He also made a note to replace his sample of scent #1055—essence of rotten eggs.

Moral:
***The sweet smell of success
isn't always dollars and scents.***

 # 5 High-Level Assignment

Looking up at Saint Peter, Oscar Overbright said, "Since I've been here only two months, I don't want my suggestions to be construed as critical."

Saint Peter looked down and nodded.

"For example," Oscar continued, "on earth there's a misunderstanding about the difference between angels, guardian angels, archangels, seraphim, and cherubim. Now, to my surprise, I find that up here the distinction isn't any clearer. However, I have a plan to clarify this confusion."

"Well, perhaps," Saint Peter said with a smile, "this will clear up in a matter of time."

Oscar kept talking. "Another thought I have is that in any organization, it's a waste not to utilize the talents of the best people you have."

"We do try to take advantage of our gifted people," Saint Peter explained. "You will notice that Leonard Bernstein is now part of the music department, headed by Beethoven. Albert Schweitzer and

Madame Curie are codirectors of medical research. And our scientific endeavors are run by Albert Einstein and Tom Edison."

"And now you have me," Oscar said modestly. "As you must know, I was a recognized genius in the field of corporate management."

Saint Peter cocked his head to one side and delevitated.

"I'm not one to brag," boasted Oscar, "but on earth, I handled all kinds of management problems such as fiscal matters, government procurement, strategic planning, expansion of market share. You name it, and I could do it. So what I'm driving at is that, since you have me here, why not use my talents to get things in top shape?"

Saint Peter confessed that management was not one of his strong suits.

"That's not unusual," Oscar said. "On earth, lots of top executives have the same problem. That's why I was in such demand. You can't name the CEO of a *Forbes* 300 corporation who didn't rely on my advice. Everyone read my books and attended my seminars." He looked down and sighed. "I wonder how they're going to survive without me."

Saint Peter thumped his finger against his wide forehead. "As a starter," he said, "why don't you give me a report on the 'misunderstanding' about the angels? I could bring it up at our next executive committee meeting."

"I've got a brilliant idea!" Oscar exclaimed. "I'll present it myself."

"Why not use my talents to get things in top shape."

Saint Peter explained that no outsider had ever attended a meeting.

"Better late than never," insisted Oscar Overbright. "I'll prepare a study, then answer any questions."

Saint Peter finally acquiesced.

At the next meeting of the steering committee, Saint Peter introduced Oscar to Abraham. With an abundance of gray hair that fell over his broad shoulders, the dark-skinned Abraham had the face of a gentle grandfather.

Then Oscar met Moses. Though not as large as Abraham, he had a sturdy build. Beneath fierce eyebrows that were like frayed bristles, his deep blue eyes scrutinized Oscar.

Turning to his two fellow members, Saint Peter said, "You have reviewed Mr. Overbright's report. Any comments?"

Abraham was the first to speak. "You realize, Mr. Overbright, that here in Heaven there is a free flow of responsibility among the different categories of angels. When a job must be done, they all pitch in."

"I understand," Oscar said. "On earth that's called the Horizontal Duties Integration of a Plateau Syndrome—with a dash of flying by the seat of your pants. What you need are clearly defined job descriptions. Each classification of angels should have distinct areas of responsibility, with proper respect for dynamic infrastructure."

Moses commented, "This flawed system of ours seems to have functioned pretty well for the past six thousand years."

Oscar shot back, "Complacency is the first indication of stagnation!"

Moses bristled. Saint Peter spoke up quickly in a calming tone of voice. "Gentlemen, we do not wish to be too hasty in rejecting a suggestion made in good faith. What harm is there in testing this plan?"

"Brilliant!" proclaimed Oscar. "I won't bore you with sycophantic adulation. But you're an on-line ganglion of thinkers who recognize what is endemic to angels. You've made a wise decision, even if only for heuristic purposes."

Abraham whispered to Moses, "Do you know what he is talking about?" Moses shook his head.

When the vote was called on Saint Peter's suggestion, both members reluctantly agreed.

In Heaven, time passes quickly. In the flash of an eye, Oscar was attending the next steering committee meeting.

Abraham began the discussion. He pointed out that there was trouble with the angels.

"With the new job descriptions," he said, "we are faced with bickering we have never known before. For the first time in creation, we have complaints about inequality, prejudice, and favoritism. And I should warn you that I heard a deep rumbling voice say, 'Go back to the old system.'"

Oscar replied quickly. "You must understand that any organizational change produces a minor amount of discord during it's initial application." Smiling knowingly at Abraham, he added, "As I recall from my biblical history, once before you were mislead by a celestial message that almost cost you the life of your only son. So, one should not believe every resonant voice one thinks one hears."

Abraham scowled.

Oscar continued, "Let's reduce the polemics. There's no need for dichotomy. These matters are easily accepted with the theory of transactional costs. And now that the revamped angelic program is underway, there's another area of concern we should address." Turning to Saint Peter, Oscar said, "If you don't mind, for this presentation I'd like to change chairs with you. I need to operate the overhead projector."

Saint Peter obliged, and Oscar moved into the chairman's seat.

"In any organizational structure," he explained, "accountability is of great importance. With the tremendous influx of souls into Heaven, I question your present process for measuring the credentials of each applicant."

"So what do you suggest?" Moses asked gruffly.

"I propose that we install a new computerized system that will coordinate all information on each entering soul. This will include reports from the guardian angel, observations from earthly friends, and an in-depth evaluation of spiritual values. These would be compiled instantly into a chart ranging from one to ten. Then only those with a rating of eight or higher would get into Heaven."

Moses reacted as if he had been struck by lightning. "Good God!" he shouted. The other two members looked at him disapprovingly.

Regaining his composure, Moses said, "Mr. Overbright, you are attempting to make us too bureaucratic. Even if a few should slip into Heaven because of a system you find inadequate, why begrudge them a bit of good fortune?"

Oscar frowned. "Vagueness in accountability," he said, "is extremely dangerous."

Moses shot back with a flare of temper. "As a newcomer, you may think this steering committee is incapable. But I assure you, we do a very competent job."

"In no way do I question that," Oscar replied. "However, I might add—with great respect—that if I had been at your side, you wouldn't have wandered forty years in a desert looking for the Promised Land."

Moses seethed.

Saint Peter quickly resumed his seat at the head of the table. When he asked for a vote of approval to test Oscar's new entrance procedure, both Abraham and Moses abstained.

"That means it's up to you," Oscar said to Saint Peter. "In your divine wisdom, I'm so certain you'll approve, that I propose we make the new procedure retroactive to cover all entrances for the past year."

With a deep sigh, Saint Peter nodded and adjourned the meeting.

After the Overbright entrance program had been in operation for the trial period, Saint Peter summoned Oscar to his office. Oscar marched in with an air of confidence.

"Please be seated, Mr. Overbright," Saint Peter said. adjusting his halo as he tried to find the right words. "We have put your plan into effect. It has shown us some astounding facts."

"I'm not surprised," Oscar said.

"As you recall," Saint Peter said hesitatingly, "you recommended we initiate the program by reviewing all entrances for the past year."

"Right."

"Well, Mr. Overbright, I don't know how to tell you this," Saint Peter said, gazing out over the golden sunset. "I am afraid your system has proved that you are here by mistake."

"Mistake? What do you mean?" Oscar cried.

Saint Peter looked with compassion on the management expert.

"Your system," he explained, "showed us that two Oscar Overbrights died at the same time. The other was a bookkeeper in Hong Kong who had devoted much time to serving the poor and the sick. He has a rating of nine. And unfortunately," he added, "your score is only four."

Oscar was stunned. For the first time on earth or in Heaven, he was speechless.

"What will happen to poor me?" he blurted out.

Saint Peter's voice was filled with sympathy. "I called a special meeting of our steering committee to discuss your case. You will be relieved to know," he said, "that on the fourth ballot, we decided to make an exception. You will be allowed to stay but we are going to scrap your programs."

"Fair enough," Oscar said with a sigh of relief.

"Furthermore," Saint Peter said, "we are going to

require, as a condition to your remaining in Heaven, that you quit trying to change our way of doing things."

Oscar thought for a moment and replied, "That won't be easy."

"We well realize that," Saint Peter said. "But take it or leave."

Moral:
**Even in Heaven,
don't overplay your hand.**

6 Gotcharonovinski

"This will be the first time that we've had a billionaire client in our office," Sam beamed at his two partners.

Chick, a tall emaciated fellow with prominent high cheek bones, nodded and said, "Right you are!"

Sitting in the red chair next to the window, Matie asked, "Sam, how did he happen to pick our firm?" She was a white haired woman with a comfortable figure.

"He wants a public relations firm to help him rename a life insurance company," Sam explained. "He heard about the job we did when Mellon National Bank merged with Chase Manhattan. So he looked us up."

Matie nodded her head slowly and said, "It took us two months to come up with an acceptable name for the merged bank."

"That's right," Chick agreed, looking down to admire the unusual shine on his shoes. "But it was worth the effort. Today Chamellon is a banking name that everyone recognizes."

"Now about our new client," Sam said. "We've got very little information about him. Even though he and his relatives are one of the wealthiest families in America, they keep a very low profile. Our research people came up with only a few facts."

"Right," Chick agreed. "And what did they find out?"

Putting on his dark horn-rimmed glasses, Sam began reading, "His parents emmigrated from Warsaw, and his full name is Ignatius S. Gotcharonovinski. For business reasons, he shortened it to Gotcha."

Sam studied the report and whistled. "Listen to this," he said. "He and his family own the largest candy business in America, the third-ranking chain of retail stores, two professional football teams and over one hundred hotels."

He read on. "He's a widower with five children, all of whom are active in the family businesses. And he is so painfully shy that he never gives an interview."

"If he is so secretive," Chick asked, "why would he personally want to come meet with us?"

"With a client that rich," Sam explained, "you ask no questions. When his secretary called to set up the appointment, she said he was coming alone."

"In getting ready for this meeting," Matie said, "I surely have learned a lot about the insurance industry. I've spent days studying the names of all the eighteen hundred life insurance companies in

America."

"Right!" exclaimed Chick. "I had no idea there were so many. And what did you come up with, Matie?"

"The names of insurance companies have about as much originality as you would find in a hundred acre corn field. I found only twenty-two cases where the founder had given his name to the company. Many have the name 'America' or 'National,' and over four hundred use just nice sounding titles."

"Like what?" Sam asked.

Thumbing through her papers, Matie said, "I am referring to what I call the brotherhood-motherhood words such as 'Colonial', 'Fidelity', 'First', 'General', 'Great', 'Old', 'Reliable', 'Security', 'Standard', 'United', and so on. Also a lot of companies use a direction like 'North', 'East', 'South', 'West'."

"This is going to be worthwhile information," Sam commented.

The buzzer sounded. Sam jumped to his feet.

"That must be him," he said. In his rush to get to the door, he bumped his leg against the coffee table. Looking back over his shoulder, he said with a nervous chuckle, "You know how much I count on you two, but I'd like for you to let me take the lead in this meeting."

"Right!" Chick said.

"Lead on!" Matie chimed in.

The client who made a hurried entrance into the office was a chunky man in an expensive, very rumpled suit. His tie was knotted slightly off center. He had a pleasing round face with a high forehead and graying hair that looked as if it had not been brushed for some time. Giving Sam a strong handshake that made him wince, he decided, "You must be Sam."

He quickly went to Matie and said, "Call me Iggie, and what is your name?" Before she could answer, he cocked his head to one side and asked, "Did anyone ever tell you that you look like Barbara Bush?" He then shook hands with Chick.

Matie broke out laughing. "Iggie." she said, "I like your style."

He smiled and shrugged his shoulders, "What you see is what you get. Now—no time to waste. Let's get down to business."

Iggie pulled up a chair and sat at the coffee table, motioning for the others to do the same. There seemed to be no question as to who was going to run the meeting.

"As you probably know," he said, "I'm in a lot of different businesses. The most recent thing I bought is this life insurance company in Oklahoma. And now, right to the point: A couple of weeks ago, my seven-year-old grandson hit me with an idea."

Matie smiled and nodded, "I know what you mean. I have one that age, and he can come up with some of the darndest things."

"Well," Iggie continued, "do you know what this kid said?"

The three shook their heads.

"'Grand-daddy,' he said to me. 'Why is it that you

never named anything after you?' Now he said this in a tone that implied I might be ashamed or something like that. Can you imagine this coming from a little kid? So, he got me thinking. It might be a good idea to put my name on something that will be here for my grandchildren to be proud of after I'm pushing up daisies."

"That makes a lot of sense," Matie agreed.

"So," Iggie said, "I thought about this life insurance company and decided to name it after my family."

Referring to his papers, Sam said very slowly, "The Gotcharonovinski Life Insurance Company?"

Iggie shook his head. "Too long. That's why I need you to help me come up with the answer. You see, I'm really quite a mixture. My father was Polish and my mother was Spanish. That accounts for my first name of Ignatius. And my middle name is Shure, because Dr. Isaac Shure delivered me." Turning to Matie, he said, "Now let's say that you're a widow."

"I am!" Matie shot back.

"And suppose you want to buy a life insurance policy. How important is the name of the company?"

Matie gave this some thought. "I think," she replied, "I would like a company that had a family name to distinguish it from those with nondescript titles."

Sam and Chick were busy taking notes.

With his pencil poised in front of his face, Sam said, "I keep thinking of a business institution with a family name like I. Magnin. With your first name of Ignatius, how about this: The I. Gotcha Life Insurance Company?"

There was a period of silence.

Chick offered, "Right! Well, how would it sound if we added the middle name?"

The three partners jotted this down and kept staring at their pads. No one dared look up. Gloom descended on the group.

"You know," Matie said, breaking the silence, "I go to a little Italian restaurant over on the West Side. It is called Restaurant Reggio. So the first word tells you what it is, then the name gives the endorsement of the family who runs it."

"So what are you suggesting?" Iggie asked.

Matie kept them in suspense for a full minute while she wrote on her pad. Then she said, "Why not call the company 'Life Gotcha'? The word 'Life' describes the product, and it also indicates Iggie's zest for living and his deep concern for others. Then adding his name as the second word gives credibility."

Iggie clapped his hands. "I like it!" he shouted.

With surprised expressions on their faces, Sam and Chick quickly agreed.

Iggie glanced at his watch. Facing Matie, he said, "Now that that is all settled, do you think you and I could get an early supper at Restaurant Reggio?"

Matie looked startled and pleased.

"I would love to," she replied.

The meeting ended as abruptly as it had begun.

While Iggie was waiting in the outer office, Matie came back to pick up her briefcase.

"Sam," she said, "I want to congratulate you on the fine job you did."

"Thank you, Matie," he replied modestly. "It's all in a day's work."

Moral:
Inspiration and perspiration are related by more than rhyme.*

*Courtesy of Malcolm Forbes

7 | How to Pick a Winning Stock

Roger Bluster was delighted to find someone new to whom he could tell his tale of financial disaster.

It was a rainy afternoon, and the two men were alone in the Elks Lodge grille. Roger sided up to the newcomer and offered to buy him a beer. Acceptance obligated the unfortunate fellow to listen to Roger's story, which the other lodge members knew by heart.

Roger always began with a disclaimer, "You know, I'm not one to hold a grudge, regardless of what somebody might have done to me."

"An admirable trait," commented the victim, not realizing this would be his last chance to say anything for the next half hour.

Roger proceeded with a monologue that was well memorized after many performances:

"Sometimes I still wake up in the middle of the night and ask myself, 'Why Elmer?' By now, I probably should have forgiven him for what he did. But I lie there in the dark and can't figure out how come he had all the good luck. None of it rubbed off on me.

"Now, you see, I've known Elmer Upton for some twenty years. He's a nondescript fellow, and he hasn't changed much. He's still short. He's put on weight, like all of us since retirement. But unlike me, he's kept most of his hair.

"The main thing that has stayed the same is that constant grin of his. Even when he's mad, Elmer grins. At his mother-in-law's funeral, he was grinning like a opossum. The only way you could tell he was grief stricken was that he wasn't nodding his head like he usually does when he talks.

"Now I first met Elmer when we used to play poker every Thursday evening. Like Elmer and me, most of the players worked for the Government Printing Office. Sam and Bud had their own businesses. Lots of times they would be late, and that was annoying.

"Even back in those days, Elmer was a tight bugger. We used to say that he wouldn't raise unless he had a full house. And when he did raise, most of us threw in our hands, because we knew he had us licked.

"After the poker gang broke up, we kept in touch. Several times a week we'd meet here at the lodge for a beer. I liked Elmer because he was good company. He didn't talk much. He just liked to listen and grin.

"Until about a year ago, Elmer was stingy with

himself. He always drove used cars until they died on him. He bought clothes from Sears on sale. Even though he was neat, he was no fashion plate.

"The same was true about his wife, Ida. Before they got so rich, my wife and Ida got to know one another. And it was my wife who first pointed out that something had changed.

"Peggy asked me one Sunday morning while we were driving to church, 'Why is it that Ida and Elmer seem to have so much money?'

"I shrugged. Then she commenced about how fancy Ida looked every time she bumped into her. I told her there was nothing different about Elmer. But when I became more observant, I noticed he'd changed.

"For example, I found out that they had bought a condo at the beach. Another time I commented on his new sport coat. He grinned at me and said, real casual like, that he bought it at Brooks Brothers. Now I'm not one to doubt, but after I confirmed by checking the label, I said, 'It must be nice to have so much money to spend.' He just grinned.

"Now, this sudden wherewithal of Elmer's was a big mystery to me. I knew we got about the same retirement pay, and nobody in the family had died that I knew of. So, more and more, this thing really bugged me.

"And Peggy kept pushing. One night at dinner, she said, 'Now guess what?' Before I could answer, she told me that Ida and Elmer were going to England on the *QE2*. Peggy says, 'As much time as you spend with your pal, it does seem that he would give some hint as to where all this money is coming from.'

"So the next time we had a beer together, I waited for the right moment. Then I came out and asked him, real subtle-like, where his money was coming from. He didn't seem to mind telling me. 'Two years ago,' he said, 'I began investing in the stock market. I worked out my own no-lose system, and I double my money every three months.'

"I said, 'You gotta be kidding.'

"And he says. 'No, I'm not. Everybody, including my stock broker, keeps asking me about my system, but I'm keeping it secret.'

"I waited a while, then I said, 'Well, don't tell me because I'm not interested. Furthermore,' I said, 'I think you're pulling my leg.'

"Elmer crossed his heart and tried to quit grinning. He told me his system was so simple that even I could use it. I fibbed and told him I wasn't interested. Then I paid for two more beers.

"When we finished, I looked him in the eye and said, 'Elmer, you are my closest friend, right? Now if I had something I knew was good for you, I'd cut you in on it, right?' By now, his head was nodding, and I said, 'As a for-instance, if you had cancer, and I had a cure, don't you think I'd give it to you?'

"Elmer chewed that a bit and began to squirm. Then he volunteered, 'Well, whether you want it or not, I'm going to give you my system.' Lying through my teeth, I said I wasn't interested.

"Then he whispered, 'All I do is take the stock page from the newspaper. Then I go and sit on the back pew in Saint Patrick's Cathedral. I shut my eyes and mark off about five stocks. Then I tell my stock broker to buy these stocks and sell them in thirty days, with no questions. And I always make a good profit.'

"I told him, 'But, Elmer, you aren't even Catholic.' And he said it didn't make any difference. The system worked anyway.

"So that night I stayed up until midnight, talking Peggy into letting us put five thousand dollars of our savings into Elmer's plan. The next morning, when they opened up Saint Patrick's, I was there with the financial page, and I did just like Elmer said. Then I hurried to place my bets with a stock broker. A month later this fellow sold my stock, like I told him to, and sent me a check for thirty-eight hundred dollars."

At this point in the story telling, Roger's listener checked his watch and said he was late for an appointment.

Roger put up his hand and said, "But, you haven't heard the ending. When I told my wife what happened, she let out a gosh-awful scream and asked me what went wrong. 'I don't know,' I replied. 'But I promise you I intend to find out.'

"And that afternoon when my grinning buddy and I got together, I let him have it. For a starter, I said, 'A fine friend you are!' Then I told him how much money I had lost using his system.

"Trying to look serious, he said, 'That's impossible. Tell me exactly what you did.' So I gave him a blow-by-blow account about what I'd done.

"Then he said, 'Whew, you had me worried, I thought my system hadn't worked. Your trouble, my friend, is that you picked stocks that are traded on the NASDAQ Exchange.'

"And I said, 'So what?'

"Then Elmer said, grinning away, 'I forgot to tell you—Saint Patrick's is only good for the New York stock exchange. For NASDAQ, you gotta go to Saint Jude's.'"

Moral:
Good fortune is not a transferable asset.

8 Dealer's Tale

For young Tim Adams, one whole year of sweeping floors, scrubbing restrooms, and playing the "go-for" at the Chugalong Automobile Dealership had finally paid off.

"My boy," beamed his manager, "it's time we promoted you to showroom salesman. Good luck and good hunting!"

Tim was ecstatic. Borrowing money from his older brother, he had his hair done, bought new clothes, and memorized the promotional materials from the car manufacturer.

Unlike the more experienced salesmen who stayed rooted in their cluttered cubicles, drinking coffee and reading newspapers, Tim stationed himself near the front of the showroom. With a broad smile, he welcomed anyone who ventured in.

Most of them were tire-kickers who had nothing better to do. One gray haired lady admitted she had come in because her TV was broken. Others browsed the showroom with skeptical looks: these were the "price shoppers." They made notes as they carefully inspected the new cars and departed with no sign of commitment.

A small number of shoppers were serious buyers. However, most of them were middle-aged and preferred to negotiate with the older salesmen.

Tim easily related to the younger buyers who shared his enthusiasm for the sporty models. The problem was, they had no money or credit.

One spring day, when the pale leaves were barely visible on the willow tree outside the showroom, Tim's golden opportunity finally arrived. An elegant gentleman entered and with a flourish introduced himself to Tim. He wore a tailored gray suit and had an air of indifference that implied wealth.

"I am J. Peter Westchester," he announced. "Through the media, I have heard admirable things about your automobile. I wish to acquire one as soon as possible."

Tim's heart jumped into his throat. Two other car salesmen, lounging with their feet propped up on their desks, put down their newspapers to watch.

All thumbs, Tim produced his business card, and bowing slightly, presented it to the gentleman. With a gracious gesture, he invited Mr. Westchester to inspect the four-door deluxe sedan at the center of the showroom.

After a careful examination of the interior, Mr. Westchester checked the luggage capacity of the trunk. He explained, "When my wife and I motor down to Palm Beach, we always travel with a dreadful amount of baggage. You know how it is."

Tim's head bobbed in agreement.

A. L. Jagoe

Mr. Westchester slid into the driver's seat and held the steering wheel like a captain seizing the helm of an ocean liner. Tim climbed into the passenger seat and explained the gauges and gadgets on the dashboard.

"I do like it," Mr. Westchester confessed. "In fact, I almost have a sense of *deja vu.* It feels very much like the one my wife and I rented last spring at the Riviera. For the life of me, I can't recall the make. It was one of those ridiculously expensive German models." He hummed a while then said, "I *do* like this car. Now tell me, young man, what's the tariff?"

Attempting to conceal his joy, Tim invited him to his desk, where he worked up an initial proposal.

"I suppose," Mr. Westchester said, "it is customary to try and negotiate a better price. But life's too short for trivia, don't you agree? Therefore, young man, I'll take it." Tim felt tears welling up in his eyes.

With a vague smile, Mr. Westchester asked Tim if he was married. Surprised at the question, Tim shook his head.

The older gentlemen gave a deep sigh. "I see," he said. "Well, it may be difficult for you to understand what I now face."

"Try me," Tim said.

"I need my wife's approval." There was a long silence. "Ah," Mr. Westchester said at last, "I know what I'll do. May I borrow your phone?"

He called his wife and told her how much he wanted the car. With his pleading, he sounded like a spoiled brat.

At the end of the conversation he announced, "Well, I won! She agrees I should have it. But first she insists on seeing it. Is there any chance, old chap, that you might drive me over right now so she can see the automobile?"

Tim borrowed the manager's car and insisted that his new client take the wheel. They drove to the most exclusive neighborhood in the city. Mr. Westchester pulled up to an impressive white columned home and asked Tim if he would mind ringing the doorbell.

With a chuckle, he said, "I know how to win her over. You go and tell my dear wife to look out and see how handsome her husband looks behind the wheel of this new car."

Tim mounted the steps like a gazelle. He crossed the wide porch and rang the bell. But when he turned and looked back at the street, he was shocked to see that Mr. Westchester had vanished—and so had the car.

In his confusion, Tim rang the doorbell again. Finally, an elderly woman in a pink and white housekeeper's uniform cautiously opened the door.

"May I speak with Mrs. Westchester?" Tim asked.

"This is the Barker residence," the woman replied, slamming the door.

He rang the bell again. The door opened a crack, this time with the chain on.

"Something awful has happened," he cried. "May I use your phone?"

"No!" came the answer. The door slammed again.

Tim ran frantically towards the main street. This

caught the attention of a large German shepherd in the yard of a neighboring mansion. The dog charged. Tim was almost successful in out-running him, and reached the bus stop with only a small piece missing from the seat of his pants.

That evening, in the quiet of his room, Tim sat in the lotus position with a sheet draped around him. He contemplated a monastic life for himself in Tibet. Before going to bed, he studied himself in the mirror and wondered how he'd look with a shaved head. He climbed into bed and mentally kicked himself to sleep.

The next morning at the dealership, the manager decided that Tim should take a sabbatical in the parts department. He put his hand on Tim's shoulder. "There are a lot of scams in this world," he said. "To protect yourself, you've got to think like those bums."

Three months later, during the company picnic, the manager complimented Tim on the job he was doing.

"I get good reports about you," he said. "My only concern with the parts department is missing inventory. What do you think we can do about it?"

Tim shrugged. "We have tight control at the main building. The only place it could occur would be at the warehouse."

"Well," the manager said, "I give you the responsibility for solving this mystery."

Tim accepted the challenge. For the next few nights he slept in the back seat of his car, parked across the street from the warehouse. The building was surrounded by a chain-link fence; a band of barbed wire circled the top. After business hours, a watch dog roamed the enclosed yard.

Wrapped in a blanket, Tim tried to be alert to anything that might happen. On Saturday night, he awoke when he heard the metal gate opening. In the bright moonlight, he recognized Randy, the assistant parts manager.

Randy stepped inside the yard and called to the dog. There was an affectionate greeting. He gave the dog a bone and entered the building. A few minutes later, he reappeared with two large boxes, which he placed in the trunk of his car. He then carefully secured the gate and drove away.

The next day, Tim told the manager he knew who was stealing the auto parts.

"Great," he said. "But we have to prove it. Unless we catch him red-handed, we could be sued for false arrest."

"I know," Tim agreed. "But if you follow my plan, I promise I can nail him this weekend."

Tim asked for two things. The first was to have a policeman parked in a car a block from the warehouse at a certain hour on Saturday. The officer was to race to the warehouse if he heard Tim blow his horn. The second request he whispered in the manager's ear.

On Saturday evening, Tim was crouched in his car across from the warehouse. At five minutes after midnight, Randy drove up. He unlocked the gate, stepped inside with bone in hand, and called to the dog.

A. L. Jagoe 53

Randy sprang halfway up the fence.

With the fury of a panther, the dog lunged.

Randy let out a scream. The bone went flying. Randy sprang halfway up the fence and hung there crying for help as the dog tore at him.

Tim gave a long blast on the horn.

Monday morning, everyone at Chugalong Automobile Dealership was buzzing. Tim was praised by one and all. With a show of modesty, he avoided disclosing how he had solved the case. The manager invited him to lunch at an expensive restaurant and offered him the job of assistant sales manager. Tim proudly accepted.

Several months later, Tim told a young woman about his work. She was captivated.

"You know," he said, "it's not unusual for a young person to encounter many problems when first entering the world of business."

"Gee," she said.

"You have to hang in there through that rough testing period. And believe me when I say it can get strenuous."

"I believe you," she murmured.

Among other things, he told her about the warehouse incident.

"And you actually caught a thief," she said. "How did you do it?"

Tim explained, "All I did was have them bring in a new dog."

Moral:

The enemy of skullduggery is more of the same.

9 Deficit Reduction, Homestyle

Mr. Edwards finished examining his checkbook and declared, "Figuratively speaking, it balances. But economically it's a disaster."

There was no show of interest from the other family members gathered in the livingroom. Mr. Edwards took off his glasses and rubbed his eyes.

Mrs. Edwards's way of delaying reaction was to remain placid. After a long pause, she looked up from her book and said, "I don't understand what you're saying."

"My dear," Mr. Edwards explained, "our family is managing its finances just like the federal government."

"That's impressive," she said.

"No," he replied, "it means that we're running a deficit—going broke."

Her long stare indicated they were not on the same wavelength.

Their twenty-year-old son, Rob, who was stretched out on the sofa, spoke up. "Dad is saying that we're spending more money than the two of you are making."

Granny quit rocking. The gray striped cat slid slowly from her lap.

"Sounds like bad business," she muttered.

"Right," agreed Mr. Edwards.

Propping himself up on a cushion, Rob commented, "Did you know that sixty cents of every tax dollar you pay goes to cover the interest on the $5 trillion federal debt? And it's going to get lots worse."

Granny remarked, "At that rate, I might out-live the country."

"But, Daddy," said 12-year-old Helen, who was lying on her stomach with her school books scattered around her, "what can we do about it?"

Mr. Edwards put his glasses back on. "Dorothy," he said to his wife, "we'll have to cut expenses by twenty-five percent."

She was silent for a full minute.

"All right," she said at last. "I think I can do it. But I need everyone's cooperation."

"That's the spirit," said Mr. Edwards.

"Good going, Mom," said Rob.

"We must be thrifty," said Granny.

And Helen said they could count on her.

A pioneer spirit permeated the household. With a consensus that a bit of self-sacrifice would be healthy, everyone went to bed with a sense of purpose. They eagerly anticipated the new regime of financial discipline.

A. L. Jagoe

The next evening, when Mr. Edwards returned from work, he opened the door to the wet bar.

"Dot," he called out. "Where's the gin?"

"Sorry," came a musical reply from the kitchen. "From now on, we can only afford drinks on weekends."

"But, dear," he pleaded, "I've had a hard day, and I'm really pooped. I need a martini to help wind down." When there was no response, he tried again, "Besides, if I don't have a drink, I don't have an appetite for dinner."

From the kitchen came a second "sorry".

When the family gathered for the evening meal, Mr. Edwards glared at his wife as if she were someone who had stepped in front of him at a ticket booth. As was customary, he held her chair. But when she was nearly seated, he gave it a strong push.

"Don't tell me we're having spaghetti again," Rob complained. "We had it two nights ago."

"It's good for you," explained his mother. "And it's very inexpensive."

"Where's my glass of wine?" Granny asked.

"With our new program of economy," Dorothy replied, "we have wine every other night."

The octogenarian gave a sharp hurmph! "The doctor said I need a drink every day. It's good for the arteries."

Mr. Edwards pushed his plate away and grumbled that he wasn't hungry.

"What's for dessert?" asked Helen.

Mrs. Edwards replied, "Desserts only on Wednesdays and Fridays."

"You're not being fair to the youth in our family," the little girl complained.

"I'm unemployed," said Rob.

"You can say that again," cracked his father.

"I'm unemployed—and I can't afford to eat out. I'm disadvantaged. I deserve special consideration."

Granny muttered into her napkin, "No respect for age." Raising her bony finger, she said in a defiant tone, "*Un jour sans vin est comme un jour sans soleil.*"

"My, my," Dorothy commented. "What has happened to all the cooperation you promised last night? I thought we agreed on a new era of economy."

"I'm in favor of fewer desserts," Mr. Edwards said.

Granny spoke up defensively, "You didn't hear me complain about spaghetti."

"I don't think wine is important with a meal," Rob insisted.

"And," added little Helen, "I agree to cutting out martinis."

The next evening when Mr. Edwards opened the front door, his wife was waiting with her coat on her arm.

"Don't sit down," she said. "We're going out to dinner."

He was surprised. "What's the occasion?"

"We don't need an occasion. I've already made a

reservation, and we're going to a new French restaurant. You can start with a martini. Granny can have wine. Everyone can order what they want."

"Mom, you're a winner!" cried Rob.

"I'll get my jacket," said Helen.

"Wait until I go to the bathroom," called Granny.

"What a great idea!" Mr. Edwards exclaimed, giving his wife a hug.

As they climbed into the family car, Granny hummed a tune. Rob and Helen were giggling. Mr. Edwards had a broad smile on his face.

Leaning over to kiss his wife on the cheek, he whispered, "We'll worry about the budget next week."

Moral:
Sacrifice begins at home—someone else's.

10   T. E., Inc.

"Since you're going to be the accountant for my new business," Phil Anthropy said, "I want to explain things to you right from the start. Believe me, this is going to be something unusual."

"Okay," nodded Anne Howe. "I'm all ears."

"The name of the company, T.E., tells the whole story," Phil continued. "It stands for 'total equality,' which is a long-cherished dream of mine. I got the idea back in college when I read Rousseau's *A Discourse on Inequality*. We're going to do something that's never been done before."

Sitting back comfortably, Anne laughed and exclaimed, "I wouldn't expect anything conventional from you. So go ahead and tell me about this new business."

"First of all, I'll hire mostly disadvantaged minorities. Each employee will have his or her own equality program."

"What do you mean?"

Phil told her that with their computer capability they would be able to feed in all inequity factors and come out with a fair pay and work schedule for each employee.

"For example," he explained, "left-handed people live nine years less than right-handers. So, let's say I hire a thirty-five-year-old lefty; Statistics say he'll die at sixty-six, versus seventy-five for the right-hander. To compensate for the difference, the lefty will get the same take-home pay as a righty, but will work fewer hours."

"Very interesting," Anne commented.

"And the same applies for the African-American male. His predicted life span is shorter than a white male. So he'll get the same salary as his white coworker, but put in less time."

Anne looked at her friend with an expression of disbelief.

Phil next explained that the U.S. Census Bureau found that an African-American male with a bachelor's degree earns ten thousand dollars less than a white male. To compensate for this, Phil proposed to give black college graduates thirty-two percent higher pay.

The accountant slowly shook her head.

"And that's just the beginning," Phil said. "Did you know that women under forty-five have experienced a seventy-seven percent increase in migraines? So, I plan to offer an in-house yoga relaxation program. I also found that forty-two percent of women killed on job sites are murdered an hour before quitting time. I'll pay female employees for working a full day and send them home early."

"It sounds to me," said Anne, "like you're going to have an adult daycare center. How long do you think T.E. will stay in business?"

This question startled Phil. "Who knows? Twenty years, fifty - - maybe indefinitely."

"In that case," she said, "they're predicting that in the year 2000, white males will be only thirty percent of the entering work force. So by hiring only today's minorities aren't you guilty of practicing future discrimination?"

"I don't think so," Phil replied.

"How does recognition of competency and good performance fit into your plan?"

"With everyone working under equal conditions," Phil said, "there'll be no need for special recognition."

"When you say 'minorities,' to whom are you referring?"

"That's an easy one" Phil replied. "I'm talking about Hispanics, African-Americans, Asians, Native Americans...."

Anne said, "I have an African-American friend who's looking for a job."

"Good. Send him around to see me."

"His family has lived outside Johannesburg for three generations, and he's just become an American citizen."

"He qualifies," Phil declared.

"But he's Dutch and as white as you are."

Phil said, "Well, what I have in mind is...." He paused to regroup his thoughts. Finally he said, brusquely, "Oh, to hell with it. Send him around. I'll find something for him to do."

Closing her briefcase, Anne said, "My head is spinning. I think I should leave." At the door, she turned and said, "Well, good luck. I don't know whether to call you Sir Galahad or Don Quixote."

"Or maybe just a damned fool," Phil remarked. "But I'm going to give it the old college try."

Six months later, the two met for lunch at a Chinese restaurant to discuss the first interim financial statement.

"I know the figures don't look good," Phil confessed. "But as I told my investors, you can't expect immediate profits from a start up operation."

"You could be right," the accountant agreed. "Still, you want to be sure you aren't battling windmills."

Phil toyed with his water glass, holding it first one way, then the other. "I think I'm on the right track," he said. "Sometimes it's difficult for me to make my people understand what I'm trying to do."

"You looked great on TV the other night," Anne said.

Phil's face brightened. "You saw the show? What did you think? My wife said my head's getting too big to fit on the screen."

"I think you came across well. Your total equality concept is getting a lot of attention."

"You're right about that," Phil agreed.

"When you first told me about T.E., you mentioned Rousseau's book. I reread it last week. Remember the note he made on the last chapter?" The accountant took a paper from her pocket and read, "'The ranking of citizens ought to be regulated not according to their personal merit, but according to the real service they render.'"

Phil shrugged. "My volume of mail is unbelievable. I'm scheduled for a dozen talk shows and three of them on the West Coast. I hardly have time to get my work done."

"A real celebrity."

"Don't you believe it," he replied. "I'm learning not to shoot from the hip. When I reprimanded a woman employee for soliciting something other than sales orders, I got a threatening call from COYOTE."

"From what?"

"The prostitutes union—Cast Off Your Old Tired Ethics."

Throughout the meal, Phil monopolized the conversation by talking about the T.E. concept. "I've got a feeling we're the catalyst that's going to change employer-employee thinking in America."

"Maybe so," Anne said. "But don't forget the primary purpose of any business is to make a profit."

Their next meeting took place eight months later. The accountant was waiting in the T.E. conference room with copies of the audited annual statement. When Phil walked in, Anne said, half jokingly, "Do I see some gray hairs?"

A. L. Jagoe 65

Without smiling, Phil answered, "Not only that, you're looking at a tired old man."

"Rough day?"

"You don't know the half of it," Phil said. "I found out this morning that one of my employees has hit the T.E. jackpot."

Anne asked what that meant.

"An Oriental female employee is left-handed. She's married to a Hispanic and has adopted four boarder babies. At home, she cares for two sets of elderly parents. On top of all that, she has a limp."

"So?"

"By using all of her T.E. credit factors, she works one day a week and gets paid for five."

The accountant sighed.

"Furthermore," Phil said, "did you see today's newspaper?"

"No, I didn't."

"This week I was ordered to reinstate an African-American homosexual I fired for embezzlement. The headline said 'Back Pay For Black Gay'." Phil looked at the pile of red financial statements Anne had placed on the table. "Well, how bad is it?" he asked.

Anne said very kindly, "It's the good news-bad news story."

"Sock it to me," Phil requested with a weak smile.

"First, you've succeeded in your social experiment," Anne said "Every minority organization in the country has selected you as the employer of the year."

"And the bad news?" Phil asked, hesitatingly.

Anne took a deep breath and said, "You're broke."

Moral:

In corporate anatomy, a warm heart must be accompanied by a cold nose.

10-A Tennis Reinvented

"Now is the time for innovative thinking," exclaimed Hastings "Hasty" Ace, youthful president of Tennis Completo, Inc., the major manufacturer of everything used and worn in the sport of tennis. "Why should tennis always be second in popularity to golf? I intend to make tennis number one!"

"But, how will you do it?" asked his grandmother Duce Ace, chairman of the family conglomerate.

"I'll hire the best expert to help me."

Hasty paid a quarter of a million dollars to an internationally known consulting firm to evaluate the preference for golf over tennis. In this endeavor, no stone was left unturned.

The organization sent its research teams to conduct hundreds of interviews. They planted surveillance devices in locker rooms and club grills. Countless hours were spent evaluating the opinions and spied-on conversations The consultants came up with a voluminous report that emphasized four

68   Executive Bedtime Stories

basic points:

1. *Tennis is a rigid sport.* The game has not changed significantly since 1512, when Henry VIII built an indoor tennis court at Hampton Court. Whether located in Bangor or South Pasadena, every tennis court is the same. On the other hand, each hole of golf is unique.

2. *Tennis is too uncomplicated.* It does not contribute to the general economy as does the game of golf. For example, to play tennis, a person needs only one racket and a can of balls. By contrast, a golfer must have at least a dozen expensive clubs, an ample supply of expendable balls, tees, gloves, score cards, etc. All this requires a massive golf bag, strapped inside a two-person electric golf cart.

3. *Tennis is not a social game.* On the court, the only human voice expected to be heard is the calling out of the score and the occasional shout of "in" or "out"; often the latter is substituted by a motion of the hands. By contrast, ninety-seven percent of the time on a golf course is spent fraternizing.

4. *Tennis doesn't encourage lively conversation.* Analysis of the locker room and grill tapes revealed that after finishing a round of golf, the players spend most of their time discussing the game. They talk about how many strokes it took to get out of a trap, the longest and missed putts, the best and the flubbed drives. By contrast, tennis players seldom rehash their plays or even mention that they have just finished playing.

Hasty accepted this massive document and gave

leather-bound copies to each family director.

"Now that we've identified the problems," the youthful president said to Fortee Love, head of the consulting firm, "I commission your firm to find a solution. I want you to design a program that will make tennis the most popular sport in America. The old must make way for the new!"

With a cost-plus contract, the consultants were given carte blanche to return in six months with recommendations. The project was dubbed "New Tennis."

The following spring, the Tennis Completo board of directors met at Longwoodview Country Club to receive the report. After introductory remarks, Mr. Love explained they had designed a program that would completely restructure the game of tennis. Motioning to his assistant at the projector, he said, "I think our slide presentation will give you a good idea of the changes we propose."

The lights dimmed, and the screen lit up. "These pictures," he said, "were taken here at Longwoodview, where we built nine new experimental tennis courts. The first slide is number one court."

It was flashed on the screen. A gasp arose from the Ace clan. The enclosed tennis court had a hedge in place of a net; there was a bushy tree to the right, and a six-foot boulder in the opponent's back-hand court.

"Please notice," Mr. Love pointed out, "that the players have to use the modified oblong racket to avoid the tree and rock."

"I don't believe what I am seeing," said Duce Ace.

The slide then changed to number two court. This showed the standard tennis net, but there was a small stream zig-zagging along both sides of the court.

"You will observe," Mr. Love explained, "that all four players are now using the round racket, modeled after a fish net. This enables them to make a quick swing when the ball nears the water."

He explained that with the new rules, if the ball landed in the steam, it counted as a point for the opponent. The defending player was allowed to jump over or stand in the stream to return the ball. Each player wore special wading boots.

The next scene showed a row of twelve-foot cedars in place of the net.

"This is a tricky court," Mr. Love told them. "You can't see your opponent So, the rule is that you have to shout 'en garde' when you serve the ball."

Then, in rapid succession, the board members viewed the other nine courts, each distinctly different from the next. Variations included a stone wall or picket fence instead of the net. There were mounds, ditches, plateaus, peaks, and much vegetation.

Another slide showed nine different New Tennis rackets and a heavy six-foot carrying case that would stagger a doorman. These tennis bags fit into a sleek aluminum solar-powered "tennis cart" designed to take the players from one court to another.

Mr. Love continued, "With the next picture, you will observe players stopping at the refreshment stand between the sixth and seventh courts. During the wait to get on the next court, we found there was much animated conversation. Also, it now takes three hours to play the nine courts. This compares favorably with the time required for a round of golf."

He concluded the presentation by predicting that New Tennis would be a smash. Because of anticipated demand, the courts would be busy twenty-four hours a day. The tennis shop would be tripled in size to handle the new rackets and other accessories, and because of increased revenues, every country club would want to convert golf holes into New Tennis courts.

The lights came on and Mr. Love awaited comments. There was complete silence.

After a while, Chairman Duce asked about the players shown in the slides. Mr. Love said they were employees of the consulting firm.

Hasty asked if the program had been tested on the public. Mr. Love explained that his findings were the result of computer analysis of opinion polls, and the psychological examination of middle-class citizens. Then he admitted that it had not been tested.

After the consultant departed, the board reluctantly agreed to give New Tennis a three-month trial.

The project was dubbed "New Tennis".

During the first week there was an encouraging show of participants, but the numbers quickly dwindled. In the second month, the only players of New Tennis were Hasty Ace and his fiancé.

Eventually, the Tennis Completo board decided to abandon the New Tennis project. It was further agreed that the painful subject was to be cloaked in secrecy, never to be mentioned again. Although Hasty was to retain his job as president, he was put on two-year probation.

Twenty-five years later, when taking a break during a father-son tennis tournament, Hasty, Jr., said, "Dad, did it ever occur to you that there should be some way to jazz-up tennis. I mean, something that would make it more varied, like golf."

The father's face darkened. "That's preposterous!" he said. "Tennis has been a popular sport for five hundred years. This was long before a bunch of Scottish barbarians began hitting small rocks with long handled clubs."

"But, Dad, what I had in mind was...."

"And furthermore, young man, you must learn to revere that which has gone before you. Of course, change is necessary but it must be so slight that it is hardly noticed."

Surprised at his father's reaction, Hasty, Jr., said, "O.K., Dad. I think they're motioning us to start our next set."

Moral:
Be sure your smashing shot lands in the court.

12 Skirmish of the Sexes

Lilly Valley, president of VRS, Inc., toyed with a long yellow pencil as she explained the problem to her attorney.

"Pete," she said, "it's the most embarrassing thing that's ever happened to me."

Peter Lawless, Esquire, listened intently.

"A harassment claim against my company is preposterous," she told him. "Why, I'm an active member of the National Organization for Women and the National Women's Political Caucus. Heaven knows, I dole out plenty to the Fund for Feminist Majority and the Women's Campaign Fund."

"Yes," agreed her attorney, "I recall the feature story about you in *Working Woman* magazine."

"It's unreal. I just don't know where to start."

"Let's begin at the end and work back to the beginning."

Lilly said, "John is really a very nice and responsible person, not at all the hypersensitive type. I would never have expected him to be a prudish troublemaker."

Opening his briefcase and removing some papers, the attorney asked, "What does John Armstrong do for the company?"

"I hired him six months ago as vice president to work with some of our biggest clients."

"How is he doing?"

"Fantastic," she answered. "Also he's a great team player, which is why I was so shocked to receive the suit papers. Now I find the American Civil Liberties Union is backing him."

The attorney noted, "I see that you are named in the two incidents that are the basis of the charge."

"Right," she said. "But it's absurd for anyone to take them seriously."

"Did you really make the statement that you hired him because he has broad shoulders and narrow hips?"

She laughed. "Yes, but I said it jokingly. It was meant as a compliment. After all," she added, "I'm an observant woman."

The attorney didn't smile. "How would you have reacted if he said he took the job because you have nice legs?"

"He wouldn't dare!"

Referring to his papers, the attorney asked about the cited incident at a staff meeting.

"It was meant in good fun," she explained. "At the end of each executive meeting, I give a trivial award to the person who's done something outstanding. For example, I usually select a gift in the cosmetics line. That particular month I wanted to recognize John, who happens to be the only male in the group."

"All the other officers are women?"

"That's right. And since he's so athletic—he jogs during lunch hour and all that—I thought it would be amusing to present him with a jock strap."

The attorney cringed.

"Everyone thought it was funny. John was a good sport and opened it up for everyone to see."

"As a monthly award to one of your female executives, have you ever presented a bra?"

"Of course not!"

The attorney shook his head. "Lilly, this is a serious matter. Don't you realize that any reference to a man's anatomy is demeaning?"

"That's ridiculous!"

"Under the Civil Rights Act of 1991, you are subject to both compensatory and punitive damages for intentional harassment. How many employees does VRS have?"

"Including the San Francisco and Chicago offices, more than five hundred."

"Then under Article 1 of the Act, your punitive damages are limited to three hundred thousand dollars. Unfortunately, that's not covered by insurance."

She asked, "What can we do?"

"Getting the facts is more of a remedial process than having an adversarial hearing."

"So?"

The attorney cleared his throat. "I need to have a

meeting with this John Armstrong person. I want to find out where he's coming from."

Through her assistant, Lilly found that John was in his office and could meet with the attorney.

"I'll talk to him," Peter Lawless said, "and I'll let you know how it went."

Two floors down, in a corner office overlooking the park, John and the attorney met face to face.

"I know why you're here," John said. "So let's cut the introductory crap."

"You have made an harassment claim against the VRS Corporation and its president."

"Right," John agreed. "It's good to be on the other side of the fence for a change."

"I don't understand."

John walked to the window. "Before I came here," he said, "I was vice president of Focus Computer Management Systems. I lost out because of a neurotic woman."

"Would you mind telling me about it?"

"Somebody had assigned this little troll to work in my office. She was about forty and with more hang-ups than pins in a new shirt. Then one day, without warning, I get accused of sexual harassment."

"What happened?"

"She claimed that with our first handshake I had implied that I liked her body. Then she interpreted a congratulatory pat on the back as an invitation to go to bed. Hell, I'd rather sleep with the janitor! Plus, I have a habit of staring into space when I'm concentrating. Because she sat between my desk and the window, she assumed I was staring at her. She stated this shattered her self-confidence. She couldn't work. Now she's home on total disability."

"Surely, you could have proved your innocence."

"Of course," John said. "A hearing would have taken at least six weeks. Also a lot of our business was with the federal government. This woman claimed that my harassment was common practice at Focus Systems, so the government suspended the company from bidding on federal work."

"Then what happened?"

"The president—normally a mild mannered fellow—suddenly became a cross between a rottweiller and a pit bull. I don't blame him. The suspension was costing us about a million a week. So, to save the time it would've taken for a hearing, I resigned."

Attorney Lawless commented, "You still seem to be upset about this."

"You don't need a law degree to figure that out."

"So, you intend to press charges against VRS."

"You're damned right! Believe me, it's nothing against the company or Lilly. She's fantastic. But somebody has to speak up.

Fifteen minutes later, back in the president's office, Peter Lawless looked at Lilly and shook his head. "This is going to be a tough one," he said.

"Well, at least it isn't affecting his work." she remarked. "In fact, next week I intend to take him with me to a conference in New Orleans. Maybe in

A. L. Jagoe 79

a more relaxed atmosphere I can figure out what makes him tick."

"But under no circumstance," the attorney warned her, "are you to discuss this pending action."

Two weeks later, when Lilly stopped by the law firm to sign the response to the suit, she told the attorney that the trip had gone well.

"Away from the office," she said, "John's a normal human being. One day at the meeting, there was a round-robin tennis tournament, and we were partners. We won second prize. In the meantime, he's done a great job for our largest account."

"You didn't discuss the case with him."

"Not a word."

"Keep him at a distance. He's dangerous."

"I will," she replied. "But I did agree to go out with him for a special event. We both like Wagner, and he has season symphony tickets. There's a Wagner evening next Tuesday."

"I advise against your going."

"Don't worry. I accepted on the terms that I'll pay for dinner. No way am I going to be obligated to him."

The attorney frowned and commented, "I still don't like it."

Ten days later, Peter Lawless received a letter from his client:

"Dear Pete:

I am writing to let you know that I am going to be out of town for the next ten days. It is an unexpected vacation I am taking to Bermuda.

"By the way, I have good news for you. The harassment suit is to be dropped. Many thanks for your good counsel in the way you handled this problem.

Sincerely,
Lilly Armstrong

P.S. The claimant and I were married this morning."

Moral:
***In the fight for corporate glory,
it's still the same old story.***

13 Drexel Fallout

The collapse of Drexel Burnham Lambert was like a typhoon that swept over Wall Street. When it happened, the Drexel executives ran for cover. So it was that Mo was not looking forward to meeting his old friend Charlie. At the time of his last visit, Charlie was vice president of Drexel and displayed an affluent exuberance. With the demise of the company, Mo anticipated finding a crestfallen friend.

He was dead wrong.

Mo met Charlie in his impressive new offices on the twenty-eighth floor of a gleaming Wall Street skyscraper, just two blocks from his former headquarters. Mo asked his friend how he felt about working at a new brokerage house.

"You know," Charlie answered, "like so many other people, I actually benefitted when we closed down Drexel."

"How's that?"

"Yes," Charlie mused, "I feel the net result was a gain for everyone."

Mo asked, "Are you referring to those year-end

million dollar bonuses that were doled out a few hours before you closed the doors? Incidentally, did you take yours in stock or cash?"

"Out of my loyalty and faith in the company," Charlie explained, "I preferred stock. But the kid's tuition was coming up, so I took cash." He adjusted his necktie and looked out over the hazy Manhattan skyline. "Anyway," he continued, "the overall good I am referring to is the fact that Drexel has made available to the business community several thousand experienced employees."

"Very admirable," Mo commented.

Charlie checked his watch. It was lunch time. As they walked to the restaurant, Mo complimented him on how well he looked.

"Frankly," Mo confessed, "I was concerned about you. It's great to see you so upbeat."

"You've got to roll with the punches," he said sagaciously.

Inside the restaurant, Charlie warmly greeted the maître d'. "And how are things today with my friend Karl?"

"Booming!" the maître d' replied. "Our dinner volume is up. And an early indicator points to an upward trend in the lunch trade. I'm comfortable in assuming that we have achieved our market share."

The maitre d' ushered them into the crowded dining room. After seating them at Charlie's favorite table, he presented large green menus, half the size of the table top. With dignity, he bowed and excused himself.

In a loud whisper, Charlie explained. "Karl was one of our sharpest senior vice presidents. He was in charge of mergers and acquisitions."

A few minutes later, their waitress arrived. She was a very pleasant woman with dark red hair, concentrated eye contact, and a sense of assurance. Leaning over the table, she whispered, "I have some inside information that is not known by anyone else in this room."

The men stretched in her direction.

She glanced over her shoulder and continued in a hushed tone, "There is a special situation, only available to a few. It's called Mai-Mai Broiled. I assure you," she confided, "that it is severely undervalued in price. I warrant that it has untapped reserves of flavor and nutrition."

She put her finger to her lips.

Appreciating the disclosure, they took her advice. As she walked away, Charlie said, "She was one of our best market strategists."

The meal was splendid. The fish proved to be as good as had been touted. They had stretched the visit through two espressos, and left the restaurant.

The weather had changed. Rain was threatening.

"Before I call a cab," Charlie said, "I want to pick up a newspaper."

Mo followed him across the street to a busy newsstand where Charlie stood in line. When his turn came, he and the news vendor embraced.

"Hello, Gus," Charlie said to the tall young man with a change apron tied around his waist. "How are things going?"

"Booming!" Gus replied. "Since I took over the business, profits are way up. Compared to the first quarter, there is an increased earnings ratio."

Motioning to his four-tiered magazine rack, Gus added, "Most of my inventory is junk—pardon the expression. But the demand is steady. And, if I can leverage the deal, I have an option to pick up four more locations."

As they walked away, Charlie commented, "He was probably the brightest head trader we ever had. Wharton, Class of 1980."

With rain beginning to fall, Charlie hailed a cab. Mo suddenly realized that he was enjoying a new experience: never before had he ridden in a Rolls Royce taxi. At their destination, the driver turned around to face them. He took off his dark glasses and said, "Well, Charlie, how are things going?"

Charlie did a double take.

"Why, hello, Mike," he said. "I'm sorry I didn't recognize you. Things are booming for me. How goes it with you?"

"Booming!" the driver beamed. "I sold my Stock Exchange seat and invested in a taxi medallion. I think the return-on-equity will be much higher with a marked reduction in creative destruction. So far, my debt level is satisfactory, and I've got a positive cash flow."

"I'm delighted to hear that," Charlie commented.

"Yeah", Mike said. "Confidentially, I'm working on a deal where I can get a monopoly on every cab in this Big Apple. If it works out, I'll be pulling in a million a week."

"Sounds like a very interesting proposition," Charlie replied. "If I can help in the funding and take a minor equity position, I'm ready and able."

Mike put his dark glasses back on. "O.K.," he said. "I'll keep you in mind."

As the they walked to the building entrance, Charlie looked back and gave the cabbie a wave. Then he said to Mo, "That fellow was one of the sharpest kids we ever had. Always thinking, always thinking."

Moral:
After the typhoon has passed, the tiger still has its stripes.

14 It Was a Very Good Year– Almost

Promptly at 10:00 AM, Bob Heard left his insurance agency and joined his two friends for coffee at Glenn's Drugstore. As they had done for many years, they sat at the small round table reserved for them next to the soda counter. At the back of the store, Doc Glenn cautiously ascended a stepladder to place a Christmas wreath over a mounted moose head.

Bob's companions were engaged in lively conversation. Margie Bailey, owner of a women's fashion shop, was telling banker Tom Anderson that she was positive this was going to be her best year ever.

"That's good news," Tom said.

"You better believe it!" Margie exclaimed. "I could pay off our bank loan a month ahead of time."

The waitress placed three coffees on the table.

"I've had a good year, too," Bob said. "But in the insurance business you can't count your chickens until the last one has hatched. You think you're home safe, then, an hour before midnight on New

Year's Eve, you can get blown out of the water."

"How so?" Tom asked.

"All year we get commissions on every policy we sell. This covers our payroll and other expenses. Any real profit comes from our contingency commission."

"How does that work?" Margie wanted to know.

"It's like a profit-sharing plan with our insurance companies. If they make money on our business, we get a bonus, a contingency check. But one bad accident on December 31 kills the whole year."

"What's your outlook?" Tom asked.

Knocking on the wooden table, Bob said that if nothing went wrong for two more weeks he would do very well. He hoped to surprise his employees with large New Year's checks.

"Also," he said, "I've promised the family a cruise at springbreak."

"With all the time you give to the church and community," Tom commented, "I'm surprised you have time to run your agency."

The subject changed to the year-end high school football game, the scheduled caroling party at the Methodist Church, and a recent political scandal. The waitress brought the check, and they sauntered up to the cash register. This always took time because they would stop to visit friends at the other tables.

Out on the street, Bob thought he had never seen a more beautiful day. That morning when he left home, the air was so crisp and bright he could almost reach out and touch Cat Island. In his neighbor's yard, the waist high poinsettias were in full bloom. All along East Beach, dark green hedges of yaupon were accented by crimson buds.

On the other corner from Glenn's Drugstore, a Salvation Army officer was ringing his bell over a red collection kettle. With a wide grin, Bob greeted everyone as he walked back to work.

The moment he entered his first-floor office between the 4-H and the Christian Science Reading Room, he sensed something had gone wrong. His office manager, Layne, had a look of panic. With her hand over the phone, she whispered, "It's Mr. Bertucci. There's been a bad claim. I've taken most of the facts. But you'd better talk with him."

"My God!" Bob exclaimed. "What's happened?"

"You remember the contract the Bertucci Company has to build a new Post Office in Biloxi?"

"Sure. We wrote the bond."

"Well, there was a freak twister. It knocked over a brick wall."

"So?"

"It demolished a car."

"Oh, no," he groaned.

She cringed and added, "There are three men trapped inside."

Bob slumped into his chair and picked up the telephone. Contractor Bertucci confirmed the bad news. He admitted it was negligence on his part; he should have shored up the tall layer of bricks. Bob asked about the men in the car. Mr. Bertucci said the police were going to use a blow torch to get them out. The car had out-of-state license tags.

Bob hung up the phone and sat dazed. His heart was pounding. his vision blurred.

"Well, it could be worse," Bob said in a voice with no credibility.

Suddenly he felt a rush of nausea. There was a dull pain at the center of his chest. He began to perspire. Gathering some papers, he quickly left the office and went home. On the drive up the beach, he saw only the dark asphalt of the road ahead of him.

When he walked into the house, his wife, Catherine, took one look at him and cried, "Good heavens, Bob! What's happened?"

In a choked voice, he told her.

"Thank goodness," she exclaimed. "I thought one of the children was hurt."

"You don't understand what this is going to do to us financially."

She put her hand on his shoulder. "We'll survive," she said.

"Do you realize," he lamented, "that we may have to take the kids out of private school, cancel our trip to Jamaica, and God knows what else? We might even have to move into a smaller house."

Catherine remained calm.

Bob went on. "Why did it have to happen? What did I do to deserve this? I work my fingers to the bone all year long and try to do what's right. And now this!" Looking at the ceiling, he added, "And don't think I won't take this into account when I'm writing my Christmas check to the church!"

Catherine suggested that he go upstairs and rest. He did her one better. He put on his pajamas, slipped into bed and slept the rest of the day and night.

The next morning, during the coffee meeting with Margie and Tom, the accident was the sole subject of discussion. The story about the three men being trapped made the front page of the *Daily Herald*.

Bob said it was the worst accident in the history of his agency. He estimated the claim to be in the millions. "This," he said sorrowfully, "will wipe out years of good experience. And there goes the contingency check, and all the other good things."

As his friends consoled him, Layne rushed in.

"Thank goodness I found you," she said breathlessly. "I couldn't wait to tell you the news."

"What is it?" Bob asked.

She looked as if she were going to cry. "I don't know how to tell you this," she said. "Mr. Bertucci called to say when the police released the men from the car, they weren't even scratched. And they arrested them."

"They did *what?*" Bob said.

Layne took a deep breath and said, "They were escaped convicts in a stolen car. And they were parked there, casing the bank. They were planning to rob it."

"Good heavens!" cried banker Tom.

"I can't believe it!" Margie exclaimed.

"Furthermore," Layne went on, "Mr. Bertucci said that there's no chance of a claim being filed. The police think there may be a reward."

Insurance agent Bob said with a big grin, "I really wasn't worried. As I told Catherine, I knew it would turn out O.K."

Margie and Tom exclaimed, "Bob, you are amazing!"

Within a few seconds everyone in the drugstore had the good news. They let out such a loud shout that the Salvation Army officer looked up to see what had happened.

Moral:
The job of the Jobs is to keep faith in the job.

15 | Marx Brothers

Dean Markel was apprehensive about meeting his first Rostovian. He wondered if perhaps he was being overzealous in giving an entire day to a foreigner, this Ivan Marx, whom he probably would never see again.

"I guess I feel obligated," he explained to his wife. "After all, we Americans have the answers to the problems of these poor struggling people."

As Dean waited at the Oklahoma City Airport for the arrival, he scanned the fact sheet provided by the USA-Rostovia Business Exchange. Ivan, it said, was 35 years old, a graduate engineer, married with three children. He was now employed by the state to oversee plumbing and air conditioning in commercial buildings.

Encouraged by Rostovia's new independence, Ivan now proposed to start his own firm with his two brothers.He had saved money to come to America to meet with successful mechanical contractors.

"I have much to learn," he wrote to Dean, "and I

know I will find the answers in your country."

It seemed straightforward enough. As a successful building contractor, Dean had the technical know-how to handle Ivan's questions. He had served on an advisory council to assist the Balkan states in their conversion to capitalism. Still, this was to be his first face-to-face meeting with a Rostovian.

Dean stood at the gate as the plane arrived. He had no trouble spotting Ivan. His Rostovian guest was a chunky fellow with a large face, high cheekbones and a healthy black moustache. He wore a wide-brimmed hat, square-toed shoes, and a baggy suit of coarsely woven material.

Dean greeted him warmly. While waiting for the luggage, they chatted about Ivan's flight, the price of American cigarettes, and the weather. His earlier concerns faded away, and he felt he was going to enjoy this experience.

As they strolled through the airport, Dean sensed the awareness one has when showing familiar sights to a stranger. He hoped Ivan was impressed by the efficiency with which the luggage was delivered, the neat food and gift shops, and the spacious airport. To his disappointment, the visitor failed to mention any of these. Ivan's first reaction came on the expressway heading into the city.

"This looks like Rostovia," he said, gazing across at the flat barren region. "When I was small, I spent summers on my grandfather's farm. It was very much like this."

Dean experienced a surge of pride as the skyline

of Oklahoma City appeared in the distance. His guest didn't seem to notice.

"As you know," Ivan said, "our *nomenklatura*, which is like your legislature—has passed a law allowing individuals to start a business. For someone like me, raised under the socialist regime, this is a revolutionary concept. But unlike you Americans, we are not experienced in the art of capitalism. You are a very lucky man."

With a smile, Dean said, "You're right. America is the land of opportunity. I think what a wonderful world it would be if all countries were like America." He was warming to one of his favorite subjects. "For an entrepreneur, this country offers everything you need to succeed. It's too bad you're not starting your company here."

Stroking his moustache, Ivan suggested, "Let us proceed as if I were starting a business in America. You can tell me how to go about it, and that will probably answer my many questions."

During the next half hour, Dean gave him the basics of managing a construction company. Later in Dean's office, Ivan reviewed the notes he had made in the car.

"I noticed," he said, "that your company is named after you. So, along with my brothers who will be working with me, I will call my enterprise 'Marx Brothers Contractors'."

Dean chuckled.

Referring to his notes, Ivan asked. "If I start my business in America, would the government subsidize me?"

"No," Dean replied.

Ivan was surprised. "Why not?" he asked. "If I start a business, I will employ people. This takes the burden off the state. Therefore, the government will benefit, and they should pay part of my costs. Is that not so?"

"It doesn't work that way in America."

"In Rostovia, the government will give new enterprises a twenty percent subsidy for the first year then phase it out over five years. Also, does not your government help out all businesses in trouble, like they did for the Chrysler Company?" Dean made no comment. "Now suppose I have enough capital to get started. What comes next?"

Dean explained that he would need to obtain a business permit and a plumbing license for each jurisdiction in which he planned to operate. For his employees, he must buy both workers' compensation and unemployment compensation.

Ivan asked, "If I pay them myself, why do I need someone else to compensate and make them unemployed?"

It took some time to answer this question.

"Also," Dean said, "you will have to provide for hospitalization, life insurance, sick leave, vacations, retirement, child care, and Social Security."

"How much does that cost?"

"Last year, our fringe cost for each employee was nearly four thousand dollars. Of all my labor costs, twenty-seven percent goes for these benefits."

Ivan jotted notes on his pad. "Hmm," he said. "That means your worker only keeps seventy-three dollars when you pay him a hundred."

"It doesn't work that way," Dean explained. "The employee gets his hundred dollars, but it costs the employer a hundred and twenty-seven."

Ivan scratched his head, "In that case," he said, "you are acting in a paternal capacity. In Rostovia, we think it best for the workers to care for themselves. It makes them stronger."

At this point, Dean suggested they take a break and inspect one of his job sites in the city. He purposely picked a parking garage that would require them to walk down the Street of Fountains. The visitor was very impressed.

"In two hundred years," Ivan said, "this will resemble a street in Rostovia." Further on, they passed several homeless people huddled against the side of a building.

"Who are they?" Ivan wanted to know. Dean tried to give a concise definition. Perplexed, Ivan asked, "But do not they have family and friends who care for them?"

Before Dean could answer, they arrived at the construction site. Donning hard hats, they spent two hours inspecting the building. Ivan was fascinated by the workmanship. He was especially amazed at the sixty-ton capacity of the rooftop air conditioning and heating unit.

At one o'clock, Dean suggested they lunch at the City Club. There they took a table with a view of the city.

"Instruct me more," Ivan said.

Dean gathered his thoughts. "As an employer," he said, "you will be responsible for deducting federal and state income taxes from each paycheck."

"You tell me you work as tax collector?" Ivan frowned. "How much does the government pay you to do this? Why does not the government trust the workers to pay their own taxes?"

"Those are three questions you've hit me with," Dean replied. "The answers are, 'yes,' 'nothing,' and 'I don't know'."

Ivan looked puzzled.

"Also," Dean explained, "if you don't promptly pay taxes on your company earnings, and remit your employees' taxes, you'll be in trouble with the Internal Revenue Service."

"Is this your KGB?" Ivan asked.

"Of course not."

Ivan looked at him quizzically. "If you do not do what must be done, what will your Internal Revenue Service do?"

"They can take away your property and put you in jail."

"Same as KGB," Ivan said. "Perhaps," he added, "that accounts for the fact that in your country you have so many prisoners."

"I don't understand," Dean replied.

"For every one thousand citizens, you have almost twice as many prisoners as we have in Rostovia."

"Is this your KGB?" Ivan asked.

"You may be right in your figures," Dean said. "But I doubt that the IRS can take credit for that many people behind bars."

After lunch they drove to another construction job in the suburbs. At five o'clock, they ended up at Dean's home. As they drove up the long circular driveway to the impressively big house, Ivan commented, "You got some *dacharoma*. That means 'mansion' in Rostovia."

Ivan was awed by the spaciousness of the rooms. He marveled at the suit of armor (made in USA) that was standing guard in the far corner of the family room. Dean mixed drinks, and the two men settled in next to the roaring fireplace.

After a few sips of whiskey, Ivan relaxed. He spoke of his homeland. He especially mentioned the strong family structure, the belief in God, and the warm camaraderie among Rostovians.

"We are a new and struggling country," he said, "and we have so much to learn from America."

"Don't change too fast," Dean warned.

"In setting up our government, we want to be sure it will be a help and not be a burden to our economy. We have a saying in Rostovia: 'If the ox does not help pull the plow, why feed it?'"

An hour later, Dean drove his guest back to the airport, then returned home for dinner. That evening, when he and his wife were having a nightcap, she remarked that he had been exceptionally quiet all evening.

He said, "You know what, next summer let's do something different."

"Like what?"

He mused for a moment, then said, "Instead of spending time at the ranch in Wyoming, I think we should go to Rostovia."

She burst into laughter.

"You?" she said. "I couldn't get you out of this country with a crowbar. You always say, 'Why go anywhere else when we have the best right here in America?'"

Moral:
If you have all the answers, you don't understand the questions.

16 Personal Service

"It's a lost cause," Maggie said. She spoke with the positive tone that is reserved for an office manager.

Her boss, Greg Burns, shook his head. "In this modern age of communications," he said, "I know I can get in touch with Todd Klingle. After all, he's been our contact for over four years."

Maggie said, "Well, maybe they do things differently out on the West Coast than we do here in Maine. But I've tried a dozen times. All I get is his voice mail where we place our orders."

"We always get great service," Greg said. "So when I get out to San Francisco next week, I want to thank him in person and take him out to dinner."

"The only way you're going to reach that fellow," Maggie exclaimed, "will be through telepathy."

Greg said, "I'll show you how to do it. Get me the name of the president, and I'll call him."

"I thought you'd suggest that, so I've already checked. It's Reginald Magnificent."

Greg looked at his watch. "Twelve o'clock—that's nine out there."

Using the speaker phone, he dialed the California number. After ten rings, his call was answered by a sexless voice: "Thank you for calling the Greatest Western Pacific Supply and Manufacturing Corporation of America. If you are calling from a rotary phone, you and/or your company are so antiquated that we prefer not to deal with you. Please hang up.

"If you are calling from a push-button phone, have pen in hand and listen to the following message...."

Maggie grabbed a pad. "Ready to roll," she said.

The Voice continued. "If you are calling to place an order for one of our products that is smaller than a bread box, press one.

"If what you want to order is larger than a bread box, press two.

"If you don't know the size of a bread box and need assistance, press three...."

"I told you," Maggie said. "You ain't heard nothing yet."

The Voice gave instructions up through number twelve. Then it said, "If you are calling to find out why you haven't received an order you placed within the past month, call again next week. Odds are that you will have received it by then. Remember that patience pays off.

"If you are checking about an old, old order, press thirteen.

"Here at Greatest Western Pacific Supply and Manufacturing Corporation of America, quality and accuracy are our top priorities. However, if you are calling to report a defect in one of our products, dial 'complaint,' which is spelled C-O-M-P-L-A-N-T."

"It's twelve-thirty," Maggie said. "Shall I order sandwiches?"

"No thanks," Greg replied. "This shouldn't take much longer."

"You're a born optimist," she remarked.

The Voice droned on: "If you are a dissident shareholder questioning the dismal earnings in our most recent statement, press forty-eight.

"If you are calling to report a property damage claim with one of our trucks, press forty-nine.

"If you are claiming bodily injury, call our outside law firm. Their number is Y O U   G E T   L O S T!"

Greg said to Maggie, "Maybe I will take a sandwich. Make it ham on rye."

When she returned with their lunch, Maggie found Greg listening glassy-eyed to the Voice, which had just finished instruction one hundred and fourteen.

"If you absolutely must talk with a real live person," said the Voice, "dial that person's last name..."

"At last!" cried Greg. He carefully punched in the president's name.

After a pause, a man's voice said, "Hello, you have dialed the office of Reginald Magnificent, president of Greatest Western Pacific Supply and Manufacturing Corporation of America. I am sorry I can't take your call now. I'm either in the men's room, on the other phone, on vacation, tied up in a very important meeting, or out playing golf.

"At the sound of the executive gong, please leave your message. I will reply as soon as practical. Realize that I am a very important corporate official with little time for trivia, so be brief.

"*However,* if you insist on talking with my secretary, Ms. Slate, please press one hundred and fifteen."

"Oh boy," Greg exclaimed, "We're getting there!"

He quickly pressed the number and heard a recording say, "You have reached the office of Ms. Slate. For our voice identification service, please clearly say your last name."

At that moment, Maggie, who was suffering with hay fever, sneezed.

"Thank you," said the Voice. "Now give your first initial."

"G!" Greg shouted.

"Thank you, G. Achew," it replied. "I will now connect you with Ms. Slate."

Tears swelled in Greg's eyes as he heard a cheerful female voice say, "Hello, this is Reginald Magnificent's secretary. What may I do for you?"

In his excitement, Greg quickly explained that he was one of their East Coast representatives and needed to get in touch with Todd Klingle.

"Is anything wrong?" asked Ms. Slate.

"Oh, no," Greg protested. "Just the opposite. For a long time we've have been getting excellent service through his phone mail. I want to meet Todd when I get out to San Francisco."

"I'm afraid that won't be possible," Ms. Slate said. "But we appreciate your complimenting our service."

"I don't understand," Greg blurted.

"Well, you see," Ms. Slate explained, "you're right in that Todd Klingle's voice is very personable. For that reason, we have continued using his voice mail."

She paused, then added, "Unfortunately, Todd Klingle died two years ago."

Moral:

Don't zap the person out of personal service.

17 A Tooth Grows in Brooklyn

As Dr. Cyrus Upchuk listened to the voice on the other end of the phone, beads of perspiration appeared on his broad, open forehead. Slowly he muttered, "Not again!"

Anxiety was his normal expression. With a dual background in medicine and finance, he was constantly aware of the dangers in both areas. The chairwoman of the hospital board said she never had to worry, because President Cy did enough for both of them.

With the telephone still pressed against his ear, Dr. Upchuk removed his gold-rimmed glasses and leaned forward. Before his head touched the desk, he groaned, "O.K., O.K., I'll call you back."

He hung up the phone and stared into space.

His secretary, Ms. Fortune, with her talent for the obvious, asked, "Is anything wrong?"

"That was Millie, the head nurse in recovery," he replied.

As president for twelve years of one of the larger Brooklyn hospitals, Dr. Upchuk knew the name of each employee. Though his constant surveillance kept him on the move, he was always in touch with his command post, manned by Ms. Fortune. Because of its overuse, his beeper battery had to be replaced weekly.

Continuing his conversation with Ms. Fortune, he said, "Do you remember two years ago, when Dr. Kalamity accidently sewed his car keys inside a patient?"

"Yes," Ms. Fortune replied. "And he had the gaul to bill the hospital for car rental."

Dr. Upchuk shook his head. "The press had a heyday with that one."

"It even made *The National Enquirer.*"

Sighing deeply, the doctor said "Again, it's one of Dr. Kalamity's patients, but this time it wasn't his fault."

"What happened?"

"Before patients go into the operating room, someone checks to see if they're wearing dentures. Today some goof-ball forgot. When this elderly Japanese man, Ile Suyu, was in recovery, they found that not only did he have dentures in his mouth, but a front tooth was missing."

"Did he swallow it?" Ms. Fortune asked.

"Who knows?" said Dr. Upchuk. "But I'll tell you what I'm going to do. I'll call the dental lab we use up on Forty-third Street. You get those dentures, take them to the lab, and have that tooth replaced."

"But," she protested, "they usually take twenty-four hours."

"Twenty-four hours, hell!" he shouted. "They'd better do it in twenty-four minutes."

Ms. Fortune did as instructed. She drove to and from the lab as if she were delivering pizza.

En rapido, Dr. Upchuk took the repaired dentures to the recovery room. He personally saw to it that they were placed in patient Suyu's mouth before he was wheeled into a private VIP suite. Dr. Upchuk ignored the fact that the patient's Medicare coverage provided for only semiprivate accommodations.

The next morning, Dr. Upchuk stopped by Mr. Suyu's room. With the tutoring he had received the night before, he stood at the door, bowed deeply and said, *"Ohayo gozaimasu."*

The old gentleman looked up with surprise. "And good morning to you, doctor," he replied with a big grin, displaying a perfect set of false teeth.

"Dear Mr. Suyu, I just want to be sure everything is to your liking."

"Ah, so," the patient replied. "This fine room and beautiful flowers you send me. You are too kind."

Dr. Upchuk lowered his head and touched his clasped hands to his forehead. "We want to make your stay as pleasant as possible."

"I am honored," Mr. Suyu said.

"No," the doctor insisted. "*We* are honored by *your presence.*"

This banter of courtesy one-upmanship rambled on until Dr. Upchuk's beeper brought it to an end.

The following day, when the doctor came to

visit, patient Suyu was exuding praise over the attention he had received. "Never in ten thousand years," he said, "would I in hospital expect to have such a dinner as last night. I had dish of lotus root and mochi with sake."

"Tut, tut, my friend," the doctor said. "It is a pleasure to modify our meals to suit the tastes of our patients."

"But how do you know what I like?"

"Oh, a little bird told me."

Mr. Suyu laughed. "Little bird my wife, no?"

"Ah, so," replied the doctor. Then he bowed and said, *"Konnichiwa."*

"And a very good day to you, doctor," replied Mr. Suyu.

The next morning, when Mr. Suyu was being discharged, Dr. Upchuk stopped by his room. The old man was dressed and seated in the wingback chair near the window that was filled with the hospital's gifts of flowers and fruit.

"My dear friend," the patient said. "How ever can I thank you for kindness you show me?"

"Our reward," Dr. Upchuk replied, "will be in knowing that your stay with us has been a pleasant experience."

Taking a handkerchief to wipe his eyes, the old man said with a choked voice, "Your loving consideration has touched my heart."

The emotion was contagious. Dr. Upchuk began to sniffle. "Mr. Suyu," he said, "we will indeed miss you."

"And I you," the old gentleman said.

When the nurse came with the wheelchair to take the patient down to the front entrance, Mr. Suyu stood up and said to the doctor, "There is one thing that to me is big puzzlement."

"And what might that be?" Dr. Upchuk asked, trying to conceal his anxiety.

"Matter so trivial perhaps I should not take time of famous doctor like you."

"Not at all, my friend," he said. "I insist that you confide in me."

After a few seconds of reflection, Mr. Suyu spoke softly. "Day before I come to hospital, I was very nervous."

"That's understandable."

"That morning, by accident I drop teeth. They fall on tile floor. One break off. Then," he said, raising his shoulders, "during operation it grow back. How that happen?"

Dr. Cyrus Upchuk stretched himself to his full height. Looking down paternally at Mr. Suyu, he put his arm around him.

"My dear friend," he explained. "You must realize that you are living in the age of modern medicine."

Mr. Suyu was silent while he tried to absorb this Then, as he stepped into the wheel chair, he said philosophically, "Ah, so—ah, so."

Moral:

A tooth in time saves nine.

18 Questionable Light Bill

"I can't believe it," declared Royce Ferrari, owner of Pacific Auto Imports. He was a nervous man with a prominent nose and an Adam's apple that quivered when he was upset. It was doing that as he sat in his office and listened to his accountant.

"I discovered the problem," Mac Burns told him, "when I spotted this big increase in the electricity bill. So I asked the utility company to give me a record of the hourly billings for each of your three locations."

"So?" Royce pressed.

"It turned out that the cost of electricity for the automobile showroom and executive offices was very close to last year. Same for your service building. But the expenses had almost doubled for your body shop up on Nicholson Lane."

Royce rested his head on his hands. "And what did you do then?" he asked gruffly.

The accountant nervously cleared his throat. "On

my way home from work, I started driving by the body shop. Every night I found the place all lit up like a Christmas tree."

"Unbelievable," Royce muttered.

"So I stopped in and asked a few questions. Obviously, your employees were moonlighting, using your facilities and equipment."

"Damn!" Royce cried. He swung his chair around and gazed out the window. "To think this has been going on with the knowledge and cooperation of my body shop manager. Hell, Tom's been with me for ten years, and he's the best in the business."

"Well, Mr. Ferrari," the accountant said as he closed his folder, "I hate to have to give a client bad news. But there it is. Now what do you intend to do?"

"I'll show you what I intend to do!"

Royce buzzed his assistant and barked into the speaker phone, "You tell Tom I want to see him *right away!*"

Fifteen minutes later, as Mac Burns was leaving, he saw an unhappy man in a mechanic's uniform waiting in the outer office. He judged this to be Tom, and he thought he'd hate to be in his shoes.

Tom was an athletic fellow who played circuit tennis before joining Pacific Auto Imports. Though he was agile on the tennis court, he looked and acted klutzy in office surroundings. As he walked into the president's office, he lunged forward to shake hands.

With both arms folded over his chest, Royce

ignored Tom's outstretched hand. "Sit down!" he commanded.

Tom sank heavily into the chair next to the desk. His toes pointed inward, his arms hung by his side. He stared down at the carpet.

"Tom," Royce began solemnly, "I have a very serious matter to discuss with you."

"You mean the night work in the body shop?" Tom asked.

Royce blurted out, "How did you know?"

Tom shrugged. "I figured you'd find out sooner or later."

For a moment Royce was speechless. He rose from his desk and walked over to Tom. He stood there like a frog eyeing a fly it intends to zap. "Well, what do you have to say," he demanded

Tom took a deep breath. "You remember, Mr. Ferrari, about six months ago, we went over the figures. You said the body shop was slipping behind."

"Sure, I recall that," Royce replied. "But you've corrected things. Now the body shop is our most profitable operation."

"Back then," Tom said, "I told you I couldn't push my men any harder, that if we didn't give some raises we'd lose some of the best mechanics we had."

"I remember that, too. I told you there would be no pay increases."

"But what you never knew," Tom explained, "is that a few days later, three of my top men gave me their notice. That's when I came up with this scheme."

"What scheme?"

Tom rubbed his big hands together and replied, "These fellows like working for me, and they don't mind long hours. So I hit on this idea of letting them moonlight repairs of American cars. I don't get a penny out of it, but my men make extra money. Also, we never took a Pacific Imports customer."

Royce returned to his chair. In a threatening tone, he said, "You'll have to prove that to me."

Tom continued, "Since then, I've had no turnover, and profits are up over thirty percent. You had to pay for the lights, but that's peanuts compared to the money we made for you."

Royce said in a calm tone, "Well, I don't know what to say."

"Mr. Ferrari," he pleaded, "I'll do anything you say. You just give the word and I can stop the night operation right now. But if we do, we'll loose half our men, and that's going to chew the bottom out of your profits." Tom paused, then added, "But the more I think about it, I'm convinced that's the right thing to do."

"Now just a cotton-picking minute," Royce said. "Let's not be hasty."

"Yep!" Tom exclaimed, "I'm going to close it down tonight. Then my conscience will be clear."

Royce got up quickly and put his hand on Tom's shoulder, "Now, now," he said. "What ever gave you the idea that I'm upset? I've always trusted you, and I appreciate everything you've done for the company."

"I believe you, Mr. Ferrari," Tom replied. "That's why I'm convinced we got to stop this sneaky business. Even though it'll cut profits, it's the right thing to do."

"Do you think I don't know what goes on in my own business?" Royce said with a smug expression, "Why, I've known all along about your night work, and I thoroughly approve."

"You're kidding," Tom whispered.

"Indeed, I'm not," he assured him. "I called you in just to have a little fun with you. Now, Tom, you keep up the good work."

"Well, whatever you say, Mr. Ferrari," Tom said hesitatingly, as he rose to leave.

Royce gave him a two-handed handshake and a pat on the back. Tom was almost at the door when Royce said, "Incidentally, I have a neighbor who has a Buick with a bad dent in the right front fender."

Tom's face lit up. "Send him around," he said.

Royce clapped his hands and replied, "You betcha!"

Moral:
Don't turn off the lights before you check the bottom line.

19 | Billy Goat Syndrome

At 8:30 AM, Doug Wentworth and his friend, Mr. Sage, entered the oak paneled dining room of the Ritz Carlton. With attentive service that confirmed Doug was a regular customer, they were promptly seated at a table by the front window. The room was filled with people who looked as if they could afford to be there or had generous expense accounts.

Doug glanced over the menu. He was a sturdy fellow who looked as if he might have been a college athlete forty pounds ago. Turning to Mr. Sage, he said, "What appeals to you? I like eggs and bacon—*but* you know what it does to the old cholesterol. Also the waffles are great—*but* I've got to think about the waistline."

Mr. Sage, a very dignified gentleman with an abundance of gray hair, said, "Doug, you talked me into it. I'll have waffles with an egg and bacon on the side."

"Wow!" Doug exclaimed. "I admire your guts. Wish I could join you—*but* if I did, I'd be ruined for the rest of the week."

When the waiter walked away, Mr. Sage leaned forward to face his friend. "Now," he asked, "what's the big problem you said you wanted to discuss?"

"Well," Doug began slowly, "as you know, my company has been very successful—*but* it has problems."

"Most do."

"In the eight years we've been in business, sales have grown to $4 million—*but* there's a chance we might have peaked. I mean, we have good people—*but* maybe they're burned out. You know how that is. You try to set incentives—*but* they don't always work."

"What about your products?" Mr. Sage asked.

"We have a splendid line—*but* I'm always afraid imports will overtake us."

The waiter returned and with a ceremonious air presented Mr. Sage with his full breakfast. He then placed a bowl of dry cereal in front of Doug.

Spreading a thick layer of butter on his waffles, Mr. Sage asked, "Is your business adequately funded?"

"Yes, we've got a solid base—*but* you can never tell when it might start to erode."

"How do you market your products?"

Taking a sip of coffee, Doug said, "We have regional distributors. Many of them have been with us since the beginning. They're pretty good—*but* it's dangerous to be so dependent. If they got together, they could take over the business."

"Have they ever given any hint that they might do such a thing?"

"No—*but* they might."

Mr. Sage carefully poured thick maple syrup on his buttered waffles. He thought a moment, then asked, "How is your profit picture?"

"Our earnings and return-on-equity are better than average for our industry—*but* you never know how long that'll hold up."

Shaking his head slowly, the older man said, "I can't grasp the problem. You have a successful and well-funded company. You have good people. With your effective distributors, you aren't burdened with a large sales force. So what's the problem?"

Doug smoothed the white table cloth. "I thought I explained to you—*but* evidently I didn't."

They ate in silence for a few moments. Then Doug spoke again. "As I see it," he complained, "we've grown—*but* that puts us in competition with some of the giants."

"You seem to be competing successfully."

"Yes—*but* when does the other shoe fall? I've built my company into a super sled—*but* sometimes I feel it's being pulled by a team of dachshunds."

Mr. Sage said in a quiet voice, "Doug, I am beginning to understand your quandary. First, let me ask a question."

"Fire away."

"My boy, have you ever been around a billy goat?"

Doug looked surprised. "I think I have—*but* I'm

not sure."

"I am not speaking about your typical goat," Mr. Sage said with a broad smile. "I am referring to a special kind of animal. You see, when I was a kid, I use to visit my grandfather's farm. The only animal that was always fenced in or tied up in the backyard was an old black-and-white billy goat."

"Was he dangerous?"

Mr. Sage thought a moment. "He was more an annoyance. You see, he was constantly butting everything in sight. If my grandfather put a stake in the ground, he would butt it down. He'd butt his head against trees, other animals—even me, if I weren't looking."

"O.K." Doug said. "*But* what does that have to do with me?"

"With much pride, I've watched you build a successful enterprise. You have accomplished this with a very positive attitude. However, quite often when one gets to the top, a sense of vertigo can set in. The first indication is what I call 'the billy goat syndrome'."

"I'm trying to follow you," Doug said. "*But* I'm not sure I get it."

Taking a deep breath, Mr. Sage explained, "What you need is a quadruple by-pass to eliminate the negativism that is clogging your thinking. With your business, and probably your personal life, you have developed a billy goat attitude. As soon as an upbeat comes, you butt it down with a negative."

Rubbing his chin, Doug said, "That may be so—

"My boy, have you ever been around a billy goat?"

---

but I'm not sure you're right."

"Your problem is not your company, it's your billy goat syndrome. To cure yourself, you are going to have to eliminate from your vocabulary the word 'but' and replace it with 'and.' After you make a statement, build on it instead of tearing it down."

"Sounds easy," Doug replied, raising his eyebrows. "*But* how can I remember to do it?"

Mr. Sage took a Swiss army knife from his pocket and opened the scissors. Looking across at Doug. he said, "That is a very handsome tie you are wearing.

May I have a closer look?"

Doug obliged by leaning forward.

With a move as fast as a cobra strike, Mr. Sage snipped off the small end of the tie.

Doug gasped. He picked up the severed piece of tie and cupped it in his hand as if it were a baby sparrow that had fallen from its nest.

"That might be effective," Doug said sarcastically, "*but* you've ruined my tie."

Still holding the scissors, Mr. Sage grabbed the tie below the knot. "What did you say?" he asked.

Doug looked at Mr. Sage, then down at his tie. "What I meant to say," he whispered, choosing his words carefully, "is that what you've done was definitely effective—*AND* I'm sure I'll never forget it."

Mr. Sage let go of the tie and sat back. Looking across at the waiter, he exclaimed, "By George, I think he's got it."

Moral:
Be positive, butt negative.

20 School for Executives

Frank Brown, founder and chairman of School for Executives, Inc., was going over last-minute preparations for the Fifth Annual Meeting that was commencing the next morning. With his assistant and president, Alex Rasputo, he carefully scrutinized the program outline:

SCHOOL FOR EXECUTIVES
Inn Cognito
Exclusivato, MN
October 15-18

Day one–"Pitfalls": (Bad things to be aware of)
    Deep groove complacency
    Interim audits
    Picking the wrong board of directors
    Acquisitions, bankruptcy, down-sizing, retirement
Day two–"Self-preservation": (How to take care of #1)
    Using board and stockholder meetings

to your advantage
   Selling your own stock
   Fiddling with the profit picture

Day three–"Squeeze the Lemon": (How to maximize your compensation package)
   Traditionalists vs. New-Schoolers
   Options, cash, bonuses, and other goodies
   Takeovers.

   Frank asked about the attendance.
   "Only two cancellations." Alex told him. "But we filled them from the stand-by list, so all fifty slots are full."
   "What's the feedback from the front-page story about us in the *Wall Street Journal?* I'm surprised how much the story revealed. We never publish a list of our CEOs, and there's no printed material."
   Alex said, "I think the reporter was trying to focus on the uniqueness of the school—like not having speakers, blindfolding the students, and our mikes that screen out accents, making everyone anonymous."
   "The article made a big point," Frank said, "about the lack of social contact, that we insist on monastic silence throughout the weekend and that each executive eats alone."
   "The reporter quipped that, with our twenty-five thousand dollar fee for a three-day exchange of ideas, we have the highest tuition in the country."
   "So be it," said Frank.

The next morning the air was filled with the hum of corporate jets and limousines delivering executives to the Inn. The first session began at 10:30 AM when Frank greeted the class and introduced Alex.

"For you first-timers," Alex said, "remember that each of you is both student and teacher. You have something to learn and something to give." Alex let the idea sink in. "After you put on your blindfolds, I will introduce and monitor the subject matter. When you want to comment, raise your hand. I'll buzz your desk when it's your turn to talk. Any questions?"

There were none.

"All right, ladies and gentlemen," Alex continued, "put on your blindfolds, and let's start."

Alex began the discussion of dangers "lurking the darkness." The major points of advice exchanged by the student executives were:

■ When you succeed with a new product or service, don't prolong the period of contentment. Although a "groove" is necessary for direction, time spent enjoying achievement can develop into a deep-groove mentality. The high sides of the groove make the executive unresponsive to change and competition. He or she is then vulnerable to failure.

■ Be aware that the enforcement division of the Securities and Exchange Commission is now monitoring midyear statements. Even so, one shouldn't overlook the possibility of using interim statements to one's benefit. Take advantage of the fact that they aren't audited by independent auditors.

■ Pick a board of directors as carefully as a lawyer selects a jury. Avoid activists, independent thinkers, and those who have time to study read-aheads. Consider only those you can control.

■ Protect yourself from a hostile takeover. Design your golden parachute with a diamond rip cord.

■ If there is a possibility of bankruptcy, prepare an airtight employment contract that guarantees extended protection.

■ Should it be necessary to down-size your company, give yourself a big raise to counter the corporate pressure of staff reduction. This has been done successfully, time and again.

■ When you retire, don't settle for mere retirement income. One student explained how after leaving as vice chairman, she served as consultant to negotiate a potential acquisition. The deal fell through, but in a four-month period, she pocketed $9 million in fees.

At 6:00 PM the session ended. The students removed their blindfolds and retired in silence to their rooms. The executives were permitted to watch TV until 11:00 PM. There were no telephones, and the only reading material was the *Gideon Bible* and *Executive Bedtime Stories.*

Day two began at 9:00 AM. To the blindfolded class, Alex introduced the subject of "Self-preservation."

As a starter, he said, "If you want to retain your exalted position in your company, you'd better learn how to take care of Number One. That's you!"

The highlights of the day were:

- Learn to use board and stockholders meetings to your advantage. Generalize with directors. Tell them only what you want them to know. One student told how he avoided an annual stockholders meeting he feared might embarrass him and his family. Historically the meeting was held in the home city of the corporation, so he moved it fifteen hundred miles away and held it on a Saturday of a three-day holiday weekend. Instead of the usual attendance of over one thousand, only forty-three showed up—and thirty of these were his own people.

- When one sells company stock, prepare a statement for the media ahead of time. If you sell in advance of information that will cause a drop in stock value, state that you sell your personal stock on a routine basis and that proceeds go to repay debt incurred from previous stock option purchases.

A student told how she bought stock shortly before news of an eighty percent increase in earnings was made public. Her media statement was that her purchase was made well ahead of time, before anyone knew the interim earnings would be so good. Few believed her, but she made a bundle.

- Profits are wherever you can find them. There is enormous latitude in deciding when to take gains and if they should be called one-time profits or regular earnings. When taking one-time profits, say that you are building capital to support future prosperity. But if you do it when you're losing money on your basic business, declare that taking the gain is to buy time, even though you are actually selling the family jewels to pay the rent.

The "Squeeze the Lemon" course on day three was the most popular. Because of the unanimous desire to master this subject, additional time was provided. School began an hour earlier, and Alex didn't cut off discussion until 7:30 PM. The lengthy transcript covered the following points:

- To stay in the right mind frame, an executive should repeat this mantra many times during the day: "More-for-me, more-for-me, more-for-me...."

- For your executive compensation committee, pick only persons who are wealthy, slow-witted, and possess a deep sense of *noblesse oblige.*

- Those who give a hoot about executive compensation fit into one of two categories. First is the traditionalist who believes incentives should be based on company's performance, such as earnings-per-share and return-on-equity. The "New-Schoolers" make up the second group. They want compensation linked to stock price. The solution is to agree with both sides, and work out the best deal possible.

■ Always emphasize that an annual raise is your entitlement. If a critic questions it, reply, "Yes, but can the company afford not to do it?"

■ Stock options are more lucrative than a paycheck. One should constantly strive for higher pay, cash and stock bonuses, and every possible fringe— but fight for stock options. It was pointed out that last year the average gain for executives exercising options was eight hundred thousand dollars. Even though they're correct, poo-poo those who complain that options dilute outstanding stock. Insist that your tax-free stock option has no value, but never give it up.

■ Recent figures prove that corporations in the food and beverage business are the biggest Santa Clauses. One year a sauce executive made over $70 million, a soft drink president got a fifty-five million dollar stock grant, and a soup executive graciously accepted options worth ten times his annual pay.

- Design options so that "heads you win, tails you win." If interest rates go down, your stock value will go up regardless of your performance. Should the stock price drop, either replace your option with one at a lower peg price, or design your deal so you automatically get rights to more stock.

- If your company has an attractive potential buyer, take advantage of it. Before you agree to cooperate and push the deal, insist upon a three-year whopper compensation package, with a front-end sweetener and options for purchaser's stock at five dollars less than market price. Demand generous moving expenses, guaranteed sale of your house, and an expense pool for other inconveniences.

After the school concluded, Frank and Alex stayed on for several days to wind up the financial and administrative details. On their last evening, the two men relaxed at dinner on the terrace.

Frank said, "I want to compliment you, Alex. This was the best annual meeting we've ever had."

"I appreciate that," Alex said. "It makes it easier for me to say what I have in mind."

"Let's hear it."

Alex shook the ice in his glass. With a stern expression, he said, "Frank, I'm entitled to a raise."

The smile disappeared from the founder's face. "You know our budget is set for the year," he replied, "so, how can we afford to do it?"

"But how can you afford not to do it?"

After an awkward pause, Frank said, "So be it."

"Another point," Alex said, "as you know, I also get a bonus of ten percent of net profits."

"That's right."

"Expense can vary from one semester to the next."

"Agreed."

"Therefore," Alex said, "to assure my peace of mind, which is important to the future success of School for Executives, I'll be more relaxed and productive if my bonus were ten percent of income, rather than net profits."

Frank looked at his chief executive in disbelief. He squirmed.

Alex continued, "And in regard to my options...."

Moral:
**Executive ego and greed
should not exceed
corporate need.**

21 Assolds

When Andy came out on the deck with a pitcher of martinis, he said, "Nick, as a successful executive, you will be interested in my current project. I modestly predict that I will be making a valuable contribution to all businesses in America."

Nick chuckled. "What does a retired professor know about the world of business?"

"A good deal more than you think," he replied. "Hear me out."

Loosening his tie, Nick settled back in his chair. Based on many years of conversation with this special friend, he knew it was going to be good.

Andy poured the drinks and sat in the armchair that his large body completely filled.

"Now this is it," he said. "In an attempt to give new flavor to the English language, I am dusting off some very valuable words that have been buried by centuries of neglect."

"Where did you find them?"

"A good question," Andy replied. "When the

Oxford English Dictionary was revised in 1890, the editors dropped three thousand words, which I have been evaluating. One of them I intend to resurrect and promote in the business world is 'assold.'"

"How's that again?"

Andy spelled it slowly and said, "This particular word is descended from the West Saxon form. It was commonly used in the fifteenth century, especially in the Cotswold region."

Nick asked what it meant.

"Originally 'assold' was a derivation of the term 'olde ass,' which referred to a jackass with a very unfavorable personality."

Andy took a generous sip of his martini. "For example, the diary of a Fairford man in 1471 describes an assold as an animal with an exalted opinion of itself. Another document from the British Museum uses the term to mean a jackass with an extremely low I.Q., which thinks only of itself and ignores other animals." Nick said he saw no relevance to the business world.

"That's where you are wrong," Andy countered. "I'm initiating a program to label as assold any executive who doesn't answer letters. Even though this miserable creature is usually vastly overpaid, he has such an exaggerated sense of importance that he feels justified in not replying to correspondence."

In defense of his fellow executives, Nick said perhaps the volume of mail might be too great.

"Baloney!" Andy exclaimed. "In this age of computers, even congresspersons, who are not noted for their acumen, are smart enough to reply to bushels of letters within twenty-four hours."

He paused for a moment, then added, "It would be a sad commentary on the quality of American products to think that corporate officials become assolds because they get too many complaint letters to answer."

Nick contemplated his martini.

"In an article I am preparing, I will give examples of current-day assolds. Two of them are top officers at Ford Motor Company."

"Why did you pick them?"

"Some time ago, a friend of mine came up with a terrific idea on how to compete with Japanese auto imports. So he sent his proposal to the Big Three auto makers."

"What happened?"

"General Motors responded promptly, but the two assolds at Ford ignored it. At Chrysler, Mr. Iacocca's secretary sent a note saying how important he was and that he was much too busy to reply. So he qualifies as a quasi-assold."

There were other examples. Andy showed Nick a letter sent to the chairman of General Electric. It involved a year-old gas stove that was not working properly and that the G.E. repair people couldn't fix. In a final attempt to get help, the stove owner had written to the chairman:

We had accepted the fate of this delinquent oven as if it were a slow-witted relative. However, when enjoying your excellent G.E. exhibit at EPCOT, I thought it would be worth one last effort to find a solution.

Nick put down the letter and asked, "Did your friend get an answer?"

"No. But a month later, the assold chairman had a flunky send a reply saying that someone would soon be contacting the stove owner. Two years later, he's still waiting."

Nick shook his head and began fingering for the olive in his drink.

"There are also assolds in the media," Andy said. "A while back, I wrote *Time* magazine, explaining I was canceling my thirty-year subscription because I objected to their using magazine cover pictures for propaganda."

"No answer?"

"Real assolds," Andy said, shaking his head. "Had they acknowledged, I would have continued my subscription. Instead, *Time* sent me a dozen computerized notices, pleading with me to renew, each with an added inducement. But I'm holding off until they offer a free weekend in New York."

Nick tried to change the subject. Sensing this, Andy said, "I will end with one amusing incident that my uncle told me."

The story involved a railroad president back in the days when pullman travel was in vogue. A passenger had written complaining that he found a bedbug in his berth.

Even though this was when every letter had to be hand-typed, the fellow received a prompt reply from the president. First, he expressed appreciation to the passenger for having brought the matter to his attention. He said he was in a state of shock because this was the first time such a thing had ever happened.

To correct the problem, they isolated the particular sleeping car the man had occupied, took it out of service and had it thoroughly fumigated. The president ended his letter by thanking the man profusely, and saying that the railroad looked forward to his continued patronage.

With a twinkle in his eye, Andy laughed and said, "Although the letter was effective, when the envelope was opened, a small slip fell out. It was the president's note to his secretary saying, 'Send this fellow the bed bug letter.'"

Nick put forward his empty glass as his host picked up the martini pitcher. "By the way, Andy," he said, "I don't recall your having answered my last letter."

Moral:
If you show no response, you'll have nothing to show.

22 Boomerang

Stu Murphy knew instantly that his wife, Eunice, had taken on a new "cause." Her expression was a dead giveaway. He called it "the billy stick with a velvet cover."

"What are you doing?" she asked. Her question told him she was building towards something. In the twenty-four years she had worked with her husband running the famed Murphy's Seafood House, founded by Stu's grandfather, she knew that on Thursday afternoons Stu worked on the menus. When he didn't answer her, she lowered the boom.

"Stu," she said, "we will no longer use Kimble's Fish Supply House."

"What the hell are you talking about?"

Eunice stood in the center of the room and leaned slightly forward as if facing a strong wind.

"As you know," she said, "I'm president of FFA— the Fairness-For-All organization. And since we've not yet hired our executive director, I've spent a lot of time keeping it on track."

"I know," Stu said.

"Our goal is to get businesses to hire at least one disadvantaged person in a managerial position. But Kimble's refuses to cooperate, so today I told my directors that Murphy's would no longer buy from Kimble's."

"You did *what?*" he exclaimed.

Talking fast, Eunice said, "The best way to achieve social change is to apply economic pressure."

Stu took a deep breath and let it out as if he were releasing steam. "Are you telling me that you're applying a sanction against Ted Kimble because he won't let you tell him who to hire?"

"That's right," she said.

"You know he has the best fish and the best service. That's why we give him our business. Ted doesn't try to tell me how to run my restaurant. Why should I tell him how to run his fish house?"

Eunice explained how the FFA had placed with Kimble's a disadvantaged man named Ernest. Three weeks later, they fired him, stating he was incompetent.

"I would have done the same thing," Stu said.

"That's beside the point," Eunice went on. "We at FFA refuse to take this lying down. I've already notified Kimble's that you will not buy from them until they rehire Ernest."

Eunice sat back and waited for her husband's reaction. It was slow in coming. Then it erupted.

"Hell, Eunice! That means that we'll have to use

Acme Suppliers. You know they have inferior seafood, and they're way overpriced."

"Now, Stu, you listen to me. I know it's not easy, but you have to back me up. I told the board you would. Besides," she added, "you should be proud to set an example."

Stu put his head between his hands. "We can't afford to raise our prices. If our food cost goes above thirty-nine percent, we have to cut expenses to show a profit."

"Well," she said, "since it's for a good cause, we can afford a slight reduction. It'll pay off in the end."

"And I know who's end is going to get it good and hard."

Two months later, Eunice walked into the restaurant office with an air of victory.

"Well," she announced to her husband, "we did it!"

"Did what?" Stu asked.

"Kimble's rehired Ernest!"

Softly clapping her hands together, she told him that Ted Kimble admitted he had done it because he needed their business.

Stu cringed. "I think I know what's coming, but I'm afraid to ask."

"So, I told Ted," Eunice said, "that you would start using him again."

"But I'm happy with Acme. They're doing a good job."

Eunice said quietly, "A deal's a deal. I'm sure it'll work out."

A. L. Jagoe

Rubbing his forehead, Stu said, "You know, Eunice, sometimes I wish you would...."

"Yes?" she asked.

"Aw, forget it."

The following week, Stu met Ernest face-to-face. As Kimble's new driver and service representative, he paid Stu a visit. The meeting did not go well. Stu gave Eunice an ear-full of his impression of Ernest.

"The jerk acted like he was doing me a favor to sell us fish. If he wasn't your FFA buddy, I would have thrown him out of my office."

In a motherly voice, Eunice said, "Now, Stu, you've got to remember that Ernest is disadvantaged."

At breakfast the next morning, Eunice had an answer to the Ernest problem. "You made it quite evident," she said, "that you have a definite personality clash with Ernest. Now face it. You have no compassion. From now on, I'll handle all dealings with Kimble's."

"Be my guest," Stu replied.

They decided that Stu would give Eunice the purchase orders, and she would call Kimble's. She also would receive and inspect the shipments. Later that morning, Eunice called to inform Ted Kimble.

"That's fine with me," he said. "The only job Ernest has is to service your account."

"Isn't that unusual?" Eunice asked. "I thought your drivers usually handled many customers."

"They do. But Ernest has his limitations. *You especially* should know that."

Eunice didn't tell her husband about this conversation.

As the weeks went by, Stu noticed a change in his wife. When he complained about a late seafood delivery or a mix-up in the orders, she was overly defensive. Once he commented that Kimble's fish had never been raunchier.

Eunice snapped back, "You have a poor memory."

He observed that she was spending less time on FFA matters. When he mentioned this, she explained they had "slack time" during the summer. Also the board of directors was no longer interviewing for a new executive director. A headhunter was hired to do the job for them.

One day, Stu found Eunice on the verge of tears. She was standing in the storage area checking the Kimble delivery boxes. Talking loudly to herself and anyone else within hearing range, she cried, "Everything here is wrong! That idiot!"

Stu asked what was wrong. She turned and glared at him. He made a quick retreat to his office.

Then catastrophe struck. One evening in late August, customers complained about the baked sea bass. Over the next twenty-four hours, the restaurant was notified of nineteen cases of food poisoning.

In the investigation by the insurance company, it was found that the frozen shipment of fish was in good condition when it left Kimble's. However, Ernest admitted stopping by his girlfriend's house to drop off a few fish from the Murphy's delivery. He stayed longer than anticipated and left the box of sea bass on the sidewalk, where it thawed. He put it back in the freezer compartment.

"Now what do we do?" Stu asked his wife.

She shook her head, and burst into tears. "We can't blame Ted Kimble," she whispered in between sniffles. "It really wasn't his fault."

The telephone rang. It was Ted Kimble telling Stu that a new driver was starting in the morning. After he hung up, Stu said to Eunice, "Don't worry. They didn't fire Ernest. He quit two days ago."

The next morning, Stu sensed that Eunice had become her old self. She talked about a Canadian trip they might take in the fall. She surprised him with a gift of two expensive sport shirts. On Sunday, she prepared his favorite breakfast of waffles with fresh fruit.

When she returned from the next Fairness-For-All board meeting, Eunice was especially quiet. It wasn't until their nightly ride home that she told Stu the news. With a controlled voice, she announced that the headhunter firm had come up with only one candidate for executive director.

"They did?" Stu asked.

"Yes," she replied. "So the board voted to hire the person. I had to abstain."

"Why was that?"

"They hired Ernest."

Moral:

Be aware—the big stick you throw may be a boomerang.

23 Executive Toys

From an elevated chair that exaggerated her diminutive size, Madame Dingbatt, president of Dingbatt Toys, placed her knitting on the conference table and declared, "There ees a devil among us!"

Mickey Raton, her grandson and vice president of Product Development, asked in his squeaky voice what she was referring to. Madame Dingbatt replied, "Someone ees spilling zee beans to our competitor. There ees a snake in zee bushes!"

Mickey glanced at the other two members of the Selection Committee. Richard Tracy, vice president and treasurer, responded with a shrug. Barbee Watson, vice president and chief operations officer, raised her eyebrows.

"We will get back to eet," Madame Dingbatt said. "Now, let us see zee new products."

Following the tradition of the annual selection meeting, Madame Dingbatt would ask for a vote of approval on each new toy. Although she respected the opinions of each committee member, it was

A. L. Jagoe

understood that she alone exercised veto power.

She had supervised every facet of the company since her husband's death many years ago. When the young couple came to America as newlyweds, she knitted tiny dresses for the dolls that her husband carved. Even though the Dingbatt Company was now the largest toy manufacturer in the country, she continued to knit. Whenever she put down her knitting, it was an indication of trouble.

Mickey announced he had an entirely new line of toys for their consideration. "As you know," he said, "our sales last year exceeded $500 million. However, we can't be complacent. We must constantly strive to discover new markets. This year, I propose we introduce toys for business executives. After all," he added, "they're entitled to a bit of fun in their lives."

With her head slightly tilted, Madame Dingbatt gave a nod of approval. Mickey displayed the fifty-dollar range of toys: coin banks designed to look like real people. "This first one," he explained, "is a banker. Notice what happens when I insert a coin in the slot." The head of the banker doll moved horizontally from one side to the other.

"Next, I have the salesman," Mickey explained. When he dropped in a coin, the head nodded agreeably.

"And the third," he said, "is a business consultant." When he inserted the coin, the head rotated in a circular movement.

"I don't get it," commented Richard Tracy. "With

the banker toy, the movement says 'no'. The salesman says 'yes'. But with the consultant, I can't figure out what it's saying."

"Precisely," Mickey said. "Now for the *pièce de resistance*."

Madame Dingbatt smiled.

"Just as Neiman Marcus each year offers their one very elegant present," Mickey said, "this will be our most expensive toy. It will sell for ten thousand dollars."

"At that price," Richard said in a sober tone, "it had better be good."

"It is," Mickey assured him. Like a magician, he swished off the cover to display a three-foot-high doll on a miniature executive chair. "I give you the toy I have named Cee-E-Oh, the unisex companion doll for the corporate president who has everything."

He proudly pointed out details such as the doll's tailored suit, fashioned by a prominent Italian designer. The tiny watch was a genuine Rolex; the shoes were by Bally, and the stickpin was a real diamond.

"Yes," commented Madame Dingbatt. "But what does eet do?"

Mickey said, "First, let me tell you more. Inside this small treasure are five tiny motors that control its facial gestures and body language. And at the center is the world's smallest computer with a twenty-four gigabyte disk drive assembly."

"Very impressive," said Madame Dingbatt.

"There ees a devil among us!" Madame Dingbat exclaimed.

"For our demonstration," Mickey said, "I have programmed into Cee-E-Oh all the financial and historical information about our company. Also I have added economic summaries and forecasts from the Federal Reserve Board. Lastly, thanks to a team of Stanford University psychologists, this doll has the human traits of a typical American corporate leader."

"Unbelievable!" Barbee exclaimed.

"Now," Mickey continued, "see what happens when I turn on the power."

He did, and the doll sprang into action. Its eyes fixed on each one at the table. Settling its gaze on the president, it said in a clear and sexless voice, "Good afternoon, Madame Dingbatt."

Mickey encouraged them to quiz Cee-E-O. Richard thought for a moment and asked for a rundown on last year's sales. The doll gave the exact figure, and added that it was a thirteen percent increase over the previous year.

"Outstanding!" Barbee cried. "And what do you predict for the coming year?"

With a frown on its tiny face, Cee-E-Oh replied that the company's projections were too high, because they had not taken into account a change in the general economy, the large influx of less expensive imports, and increased competition from the Acme Toy Company.

"Unfortunately," the doll predicted, "I think the Dingbatt Company has peaked and will begin a slow but steady decline."

Richard asked Cee-E-Oh what actions it would advise for the future. Without hesitation, the doll recommended selling out to the Acme Company.

Before the gasps had subsided, it gave its reasons. Even though Acme was much smaller, it had strong financial backing. The toy lines were compatible, and both companies would benefit from a merger. Then the doll said Acme already was preparing such an agreement for their consideration.

Madame Dingbatt asked the doll, "How ees it you have so much information about zee Acme

Company?"

Ignoring the question, Cee-E-Oh continued. "With the proposed offer, each of you will be well compensated with a five-year salary guarantee and attractive stock options. However, Acme will want to appoint a new president of the Dingbatt subsidiary."

Barbee put her hand to her mouth and whispered, "I can't believe I'm listening to a doll."

Madame Dingbatt again pressed Cee-E-Oh on how it knew so much about Acme.

Crossing its arms, the doll boasted that it was superior to a human in that it could function twenty-four hours a day without rest. During the early morning hours, it had made contact with the Acme computer. Through this secret networking, the doll originated on-going communications with the Acme executives.

"Let's face the facts," Cee-E-Oh said to Madame Dingbatt. "You are ninety-one years old. It is time for you to step down and do your knitting in a retirement setting. Under the new plan, you will be given the title of honorary president."

"And who will be the new president?" Richard asked.

Pushing its hair to one side, Cee-E-Oh admitted that the Acme team had asked it to serve as president, "After all," the doll said, "who is more qualified?"

Madame Dingbatt quickly rose from her seat. With the speed of an expert swordswoman, she thrust one of her knitting needles into Cee-E-Oh's ear. The doll gave a mechanical cry and melted into a glob of twisted metal.

To her astounded executives, Madame Dingbatt proclaimed with pride, "I have discovered and keeled zee devil."

She then declared the meeting to be ended. With an air of triumph, she left the room.

Mickey sat despondently with his head in his hands. Looking at the remains of Cee-E-Oh, he cried, "Think of the research, the expense, the intelligence—now it's all gone!"

"Don't grieve," Barbee said, placing her hand on his shoulder. "If that doll had been as smart as you think, it never would have made a tactless remark about a lady's age."

Moral:
Don't toy around with devilish devices.

24 Sinful Businessman

On a late, dreary evening, a taxi came to a stop in front of the High Temple of Government, Department of Confessions. With an umbrella for protection from the driving rain, a middle-aged man got out and slowly mounted the eighty-five steps. He passed the marble columns and went through the twelve-foot bronze doors into the monolithic lobby.

The receptionist seated behind a broad mahogany desk on a raised platform was of indeterminate age, sex, color, religion and national origin. Glowering down at him, the receptionist asked what he wanted.

"I have something to confess," stammered the businessman. "I need absolution."

"Fill out these forms," said the receptionist with a heavy sigh. "Give your social security number, date of birth, height of grandfather, preference of ice cream and other pertinent information. You will be called promptly into a confessional."

The person yawned and pressed a button. A

sheath of papers ejected at the businessman's feet. Two hours later, he was ushered by a functionary into a dark, enclosed cubicle. He knelt before a screen of interwoven red tape. From behind the screen came a mighty voice. "Speak, my son."

"I have sinned," cried the businessman.

"I assumed that," replied the Voice, "otherwise you would not be here. Tell me the nature of your sin."

"I have made a profit."

From behind the red screen came a groan of anguish. "Are you sure you have complied with the many devices your government is constantly inventing to keep you from this sin?"

"Yes, I think so."

"What about the Employee Retirement Income Security Act?"

"Our employee benefit program conforms with ERISA."

"Yes, but what about the hundreds of regulations under the Occupational Safety and Health Administration?"

"We passed the OSHA inspection with no complaints."

The gloom of the confessional seemed to become even gloomier. The Voice continued: "What about Affirmative Action? Environmental impact? The Longshoreman's Act? Unemployment Compensation? The Americans With Disabilities Act?"

"No problem," the man replied.

"And *still* you made a profit."

"I am afraid so. I'm truly sorry."

"You say you are," the Voice growled. "Yet deep down, are you not gloating? After all, you have defied and fowled up your own government!"

"I regret terribly what I've done."

"Without your government's constant effort to build barriers and obstacles, the free enterprise system would be like a wild river overflowing its banks. Don't you realize that as your business succeeds and grows, you are placing a burden on your government to add more regulations?"

"That's true."

With exasperation the Voice asked, "Did not the time, expense, and cost of legal assistance necessary to comply with dozens of government regulations help to reduce your profits?"

"Yes," the businessman replied. "Unfortunately, we have management controls that compensate for these factors."

There followed another period of silence so deep that the businessman could hear his own heartbeat. The Voice said slowly, "In spite of your vulnerability to sin, your government will not abandon you. We will continue to devise additional safeguards and formulate new nit-picking disciplines to keep you from sinning."

"Yes," the man replied. "I know that to be a fact."

"Do not forget that your government is personally interested in you. We carefully monitor your every move. Like a mother hen with her chicks, we watch over you day and night so that you do not fall into sinful ways. We are here to help... help... help... help... help...."

The Voice kept repeating itself in monotone.

Immediately, an assistant undersecretary for the Department of Confessions, three GS-14s, two consultants, and a maintenance man hurried behind the screen. The Voice fell silent.

Fifteen minutes later, the assistant undersecretary emerged and reported, "According to the tape, you completed your confession but did not receive absolution."

"Tape?" the businessman said.

"Of course. How else could we keep a permanent account of your wrong-doings?"

"You mean that I've been talking to a stupid machine?"

"Definitely not," corrected the assistant undersecretary. "Your government spent billions to develop this personalized confessional computer program. It's purpose is to serve you better."

"You're too kind," said the businessman.

The government official continued, "As I explained, you had not yet received the penance necessary for your absolution."

"That is correct," the businessman agreed.

The assistant undersecretary handed him a ream of papers. "Your assignment will be to complete these forms and return with ten copies of each within five working days."

"What do these pertain to?" the man asked.

"What difference does it make?" replied the official. "For a business person, completing any government form is an act of penance."

Suddenly the businessman assumed a wide stance, closed his eyes and stood rigid as stone. Gradually he began to quiver like a volcano warning of an eruption. He opened his eyes and said with a roar loud enough to be heard by even a deaf senator, "Take back your damned forms!"

Pressing the beeper MAY DAY button, the official asked, "Are you declaring disobedience against your own government?"

"Call it what you like," the businessman shouted. "I've had it!"

Looking for reinforcement that was nowhere in sight, the assistant undersecretary said, "Don't waste your time trying to fight us. In the past decade, the only thing that has grown faster than pollution and the national debt is the number of government employees. Whether you know it or not, we've got you outnumbered."

In exasperation, the businessman turned on his heels and quickly left. As he made his exit through the high-vaulted lobby, the Voice suddenly reactivated, and the cries of "Help" resounded throughout the Temple.

Moral:

Government prophets should not disparage those who make profits.

25 Postman's Wife

Once upon a time, there was a young postman and his bride who bought a small white brick house with red shutters. Their new home stood on an acre of land. There were apple trees and a stream that ran along the back line of the property. They were very happy.

The first year, the postman tilled the soil. His wife planted vegetables and made a flower garden around the house. The second year, a baby girl was born. The next year, they acquired a dog and a cat. All was peace and contentment.

Then one day, the wife said to her husband, "I'm not happy. I want a bigger house and lots more furniture."

The postman accepted her suggestion that she earn extra money by taking a part-time job at the Jason Manufacturing Company. The factory, which made electric motors, was located on the bus route near their home.

She took the early shift, and the postman prepared breakfast for their daughter and took her to school. In the early afternoon, the mother picked up the child. This arrangement worked out well.

The wife's first job was on the assembly line. Being a conscientious worker, she was soon promoted to foreperson, then manager. Her husband was very proud of her and boasted to his fellow postal workers about her achievements.

Because they were a very thrifty couple, they wisely agreed to live on the postman's salary and bank her earnings. It was through this savings arrangement that she got to know the local banker, a fatherly gentleman with years of practical business experience. Over the years, she came to rely on his advice.

When their daughter entered sixth grade and spent longer hours at school, the mother worked longer hours at the factory. She decided to confide to the banker her desire to have a big house filled with new furniture. But she had even larger plans.

"One day," she told him, "I want to own the Jason Manufacturing Company."

The banker nodded slowly and smiled. "That may be a possibility," he replied. "Mr. Jason is getting along in years. So, at the right time, he might entertain an offer to sell. But you must prepare yourself. Ambition alone will not achieve what you want."

"What should I do?" she asked.

"Continue to save money. Also you must learn more about finance and business."

With his encouragement, she enrolled in night

classes at a business school.

When the daughter graduated from the eighth grade, the postman's wife came to the banker with a plan.

"In addition to the money we've saved," she said, "I'd like to borrow enough to buy the Jason factory." She explained her plan. "After I complete the deal, I'll move the parking area behind the building. This will free a large frontage on the main highway to be sold for a shopping mall. I'll repay your loan with the proceeds of the land sale."

Mr. Jason was surprised to have a sale offer presented by an employee. He had been eying an expensive condominium in Florida, and a week later he accepted the offer.

The postman's wife put her leveraging plan into action. It was more successful than she had anticipated. In the end, she bought the company at no cost.

As the new president, she gave herself a large salary. This made it possible for her to buy a big house, which she filled with too much furniture. As an investment, she decided to keep the little white house with the red shutters. For a while, she was supremely happy. But her ambition grew.

Again she approached her banker friend. "Owning my own company isn't enough," she said. "I want to be the wealthiest woman in the state. Then I can buy a much larger home with a two-car garage and a swimming pool."

"Very well," the banker replied. "How do you

intend to accomplish this? The factory is at full capacity."

"I understand there's a great future for the little myton motors that will be used in everything from automobiles to computers. To extend our operations," she explained, "I'll add a new wing. We'll work around the clock."

With the support of her banker, she succeeded in the myton motor expansion, and beefed up production to meet the new orders. Profits expanded at an impressive rate.

The postman's wife bought a large suburban house on five acres with a garage and a heated swimming pool. Again she was very happy—for a while.

One day while lunching with the banker, she looked across at her friend and said, "Although my husband is content to be a letter carrier, I'm far more ambitious."

"I never would have suspected that," the banker said with a smile.

"I've proved I can do anything I set mind to," she continued. "Now that I am the principal manufacturer of myton motors in the Midwest, I intend to become the biggest in the country. "Sniffing the yellow rose pinned to the lapel of her silk double-breasted suit, she pushed forward boldly. "I know I can do it."

Their discussion lasted hours and ended up at the bank office. They outlined a strategy through which she could use investors to fund the acquisition of other myton makers. With an expanded manufacturing base, she could sell stock though a public offering.

Using the assistance of investment specialists, the postman's wife completed her financial plan. It was quickly implemented, and she went on a buying spree of myton manufacturers. Two years later, the Jason Company owned ten of the major producers.

Inc. magazine published a very favorable article about "The Mighty Lady of Myton."

The postman's wife and her husband moved into a twelve-bedroom mansion. It had a three-bedroom gatehouse, indoor and outdoor pools, stables, and a tennis court. Though it now took the postman longer to drive back and forth to his mail route, he did not complain. And, temporarily, he had a very satisfied wife.

When their daughter graduated from college and married, the postman and his wife gave the young couple the little white brick house with the red shutters.

A year later, following a banquet at which she had been honored as the business person of the year, the postman's wife met with her banker friend. He had grown quite lame and walked with two canes.

"I am very proud of you," he confessed. "You have achieved everything you ever wanted."

"Not yet," she said in a serious tone. "I want a yacht, a corporate jet, and a town house in London." She patted the banker's hand. "You must realize, my friend, there's a great fortune to be made in the foreign myton trade."

The old man shook his head. "My child," he cautioned, "I advise against traveling unchartered waters. There are many hidden reefs below."

"I still want to do it," she said. "And when I accomplish this, I intend to buy an additional estate in California. There, dear friend, you'll have a place in which to live the rest of your life."

The postman's wife then selected an Oriental country that was eager to get established in myton manufacturing. Tutoring herself for the experience, she acquired some of the new language, and learned how to bow, click her heels, and eat with chopsticks.

The Orientals were impressed. They assured her if she signed their agreement, they would take over her company and in two years increase her sales tenfold. She quickly signed and returned to America a pleased woman—for a while.

Under the terms of the contract, the foreigners had authority to put their top managers in the Jason factories. They also had the right to substitute their own manufacturing tools. All this took time, caused confusion, and damaged efficiency. For the first time, many shipments of mytons were returned as inferior.

When the postman's wife protested, the Orientals said, "Do not fear. Keep in mind the increased production and profits we have promised."

Having relinquished control, she could do nothing but go along and hope for the best.

Three years later the Orientals said, "So sorry." They returned what was left of her company. She made an audit and frantically called her banker friend.

He carefully analyzed the statements. "You are right," he said. "The liabilities exceed your corporate and personal wealth by $10 million."

"What shall I do?" wailed the postman's wife.

He gave her his final two words of advice: "Chapter eleven."

In the trying years which followed, the daughter's husband accepted a new job, and the couple moved to a distant city. The postman and his wife returned to the little white brick house with the red shutters. The postman, nearing retirement, still maintained his mail route. Every evening, he and his wife worked in the garden.

Each Wednesday afternoon, the old banker came out for a visit. On the small flagstone patio under the gnarled apple trees, the postman's wife sat quietly beside his wheel chair. They sipped a glass of wine and talked.

One afternoon, she confided, "I want to spend the rest of my life traveling to all the first-class resorts in the world. I know I can do it. We'll raise money for a new company. Then I'll take over the U.S. Mail Service—and make it profitable!"

Moral:
***It is good to stretch beyond your reach,
until you reach the edge.***

26 Fini La Vacation

As Bob walked into the open-air cocktail area, he heard someone calling his name. From a crowded table next to the piano, a big balding man dressed in tropical colors stood up and motioned to him.

"Come join us for a drink," he insisted. "Remember me? I was with you on the beach this afternoon. I'm Chuck, the fat guy in the red trunks, in case you don't recognize me with my clothes on."

Everyone at the table chuckled.

The new host slapped Bob on the shoulder and said, "Meet the uglies who run the Ajax Tool and Die Factory, way up there in Fargo, North Dakota. Incidently," Chuck added, "I'm the treasurer of the company and that's my wife, Lucy." He pointing across the table to the largest of the three women.

Nodding towards a man with a large sunburned nose, Chuck continued the introductions. "That's our vice president Manny, and Susie, his better half."

"You better believe it!" Susie blurted out. "I'm the best thing that ever happened to that dummy."

There was another round of giggles.

Chuck continued doing the honors. "And last but not least, there is good old Irv, our fearless president, and our first lady Gertrude, known as Gert after her second drink. She became Gert about ten minutes ago."

Irv looked as if he had just parked his eighteen-wheeler after a hard drive. By his expression, he indicated it was too late in the day for him to meet a new person.

Chuck leaned back in his chair. "Well, Bob, now that you've met the motley gang, what'll you have to drink?"

"Perrier with lime."

There was a hush at the table. "Aw, come on," Chuck groaned. "Try one of those rum drinks. They're terrific."

Bob smiled and said firmly, "Until I get acclimated, I think I should stick with something tame."

Vice President Manny asked, "Is this your first visit to Little Dix Bay?"

"Yes, it is."

"Gee whiz," big Lucy said, "This is our fourth time."

"Fifth," Chuck corrected her, then said to Bob, "You got to excuse her. She's got a lot of figure, but she's lousy with numbers."

Lucy picked up her glass and acted as if she were going to throw it at him. Everyone laughed.

"And the best thing about coming here," Chuck informed him, "is that it doesn't cost us anything."

"Really?" Bob said. "Do you own the place?"

"Naw," Chuck replied, "We let good old Uncle Sam pick up the tab."

"Well, that is probably a private matter," Bob said, "so I don't need to know about it."

"But I want to tell you how it works," Chuck insisted. "You see, we run the Ajax Factory up in Fargo where the winters are tough."

"Good gosh," Gert said. "Let's change the subject. Who wants to think about business when we're on vacation?"

"She's right," Bob agreed.

Chuck shook his head. Turning to the others he said, "When you got something good going, you ought to share it with your friends, right? And Bob here, he's my new friend."

"You are too kind," Bob replied. "But, I agree with Gertrude that you shouldn't discuss business."

"Yeah, cut it out," Irv said. "Let's talk about something sensible, like getting another round of drinks."

Bob said, "I imagine you enjoy this warm weather after being in the frozen north."

"Hell, yes!" Chuck shot back. "As I was explaining, we three fellows are the guts of Ajax. It can't run without us. And that's why we're here."

"Oh," Bob said.

"Hey, it's very simple," Chuck pressed on. "Every year when the snow is up to your belly button, we come down here for our annual board meeting. Get it?" He gave Bob a nudge, and everyone giggled.

"I really don't need to know about your business," Bob protested.

"We call it a board meeting," Chuck explained with a broad grin. "But it's hard to get bored down here. Get it?"

"Yes," Bob said, "I'm beginning to understand."

"It's perfectly legit," Chuck explained. "We are the company, therefore, we are entitled to a little R and R."

"I guess so," Bob said.

"So since we need a change, we make it a rule never to talk business while we're down here. All work and no play makes Chuck a dull guy. Am I right?"

"You jerk!" Lucy cried out. "You're doing it now. You're talking business."

"O.K.," Chuck agreed. "No more of that." Then he asked Bob, "Incidently, do you like our sport coats?" He stuck out his sleeve so Bob could feel the material. "That's real raw silk, and these three coats are free because they'll show up on our expense account as temporary secretarial help."

There was a chorus of approving laughter.

"Last year," Gert chimed in, "we girls got new evening dresses. So we figured this year the guys should have a treat."

The waiter reappeared with the Perrier and lime. Chuck grabbed him by his coattail and said, "While you're here, Buster, let's have another round." After the waiter left, Chuck whispered loudly, "That baboon couldn't find a coconut if it was tied around his neck."

He then turned his attention back to his new friend. "Tell me, Bob, where are you from?"

"Washington."

Irv asked, "Is that Washington State or Washington, D.C.?"

"D.C.." Bob answered.

"And what do you do for a living?" Chuck asked. "You look like some kind of a professor."

"No," Bob said. "I work for the government."

"The federal government?" Chuck probed, hesitatingly.

"Yes."

There was a sudden chill at the table. At last, Chuck nervously asked, "Which department?"

Bob put down his glass and answered, "IRS."

In unison, the guts of the Ajax Tool and Die Factory of Fargo, North Dakota, made a noise that sounded like the breaking of the vacuum on a new can of tennis balls. The three couples looked as if Armageddon were about to occur.

Silence was finally broken. President Irv said to Treasurer Chuck, "O.K., wise ass, now give him our Social Security numbers."

Moral:

A raucous bird of paradise with a gullet full of stolen corn becomes a cooked goose.

27 Wynmill Dichotomy

Jonathan Wynmill IV, head of Wynmill Industries, knew he must confront his life-long secret—the company was controlled by ghosts.

The one-hundred-fifty-year-old family ancestry of the Wynmill organization was preserved in the boardroom by the stern portraits of the deceased Wynmills. Complying with tradition, the current Wynmill had his portrait rendered when he was sixty-five. It would be hung after he had been laid to rest in the family crypt.

His dependency on his forefathers began when he assumed the presidency after his father's death. He felt inadequate, but the family insisted he take charge.

It was during this early period at the corporate helm that he began the practice of going into the boardroom and locking the door. He would stare at the portraits of his three predecessors. With his eyes closed, he allowed their silent wisdom to flow into his receptive brain. He accepted their unimpeachable guidance, and he continued to expand the fortunes of Wynmill Industries. Then came the Jamaican trip.

During the spring meeting of the Old Presidents Organization at Round Hill, near Ocho Rios, two factors set into motion a transformation in Jonathan IV.

The first was the island itself. He enjoyed basking on the warm sand, sipping Planters Punch, wearing bright sports attire. Gradually he sensed within himself a long-dormant youthful verve.

The second force was a presentation by a Yale University professor. The subject was the advantage of "open communication" in an organization.

Jonathan was fascinated. This concept had never been considered at Wynmill Industries. He took copious notes and discussed it with other participants.

During his flight back to San Francisco, he continued to ponder the idea. When the plane landed, he vowed to put open communication into action as soon as possible.

The first day back at work, he called his four vice presidents for a late afternoon meeting. In the past, he insisted upon punctuality; this avoided his having to make small talk. But today was different. He was perfectly at ease as the first three arrived, and waiting for the fourth did not phase him.

To the woman seated on his left, he said, "Sally, I was sorry to learn that you have been sick."

"It was just a bug," she said in an apologetic tone. "It was only for a few days. I didn't want to come back until I was sure I wasn't contagious."

"Things like that will happen," commented the younger woman on Jonathan's right. "You have to learn how to take care of yourself."

"Thank you, Mabel," Sally snapped. "I appreciate your concern. But if I need medical advice, I know where to get it."

Jonathan glanced at his conference notes and spotted this statement: *A symptom of a closed corporation is a constant yiping.*

"Well, well," exclaimed Stanley, turning to the clock on the wall. "Our friend Ben is late again. Bet he blames it on being so busy."

"If he does," said Mabel, "at least he won't blame it on others, like some people in this company do."

"For Pete's sake!" Stanley exploded. "I wasn't pointing a finger at you yesterday when I found that mistake in our new catalogue. Sure, somebody goofed. But I didn't say it was you."

"Indeed, it wasn't," she agreed.

At that moment, Ben burst into the room. He was a middle-aged man who looked stressed. Placing his briefcase on the table, he apologized. "Sorry I'm late. There were some last-minute things I had to handle."

Stanley shot a knowing glance at the others.

Jonathan referred to his notes: *Employees in a closed corporation will express frustration by taking it out on fellow employees. They will be overly defensive and critical.*

With everyone present, Jonathan explained that

Jonathan Wynmill knew he must confront his life long secret.

---

he wanted to share ideas he had picked up at the OPO conference. He suggested that they ask questions but withhold opinions until they had time to give it more thought. He then presented his suggestions about converting Wynmill Industries to open communication.

Ben was stunned. "Mr. Wynmill," he said, "did I hear you correctly? Did you say that all future planning would be consensus oriented?"

Jonathan IV looked up at the portrait of the first Jonathan. The old gentleman was frowning.

"My boy," the portrait said, "have you lost your mind? When I started this business in 1840, I had two partners who didn't agree with me. I had to get rid of them, and it cost me a bundle. So, I insist you keep tight control—and don't trust anyone!"

Jonathan glanced up at Jonathan II. The face in the portrait had raised eyebrows.

"You young whipper-snapper!" the revered ancestor shouted. "If you ask employees for advice, they'll think you're weak. They'll rebel and try to take over. All you need is a consensus of one. Believe me, I know, because one time, even before California became a state, I...."

Mabel interrupted this secret monologue.

"Did you say the chain of command will be modified from the bottom to the top so we can deal openly with employee concerns?"

"That's correct," Jonathan replied.

Then Stanley asked, "Does that openness also apply to financial statements?"

When Jonathan replied in the affirmative, he heard the booming voice of Jonathan III: "Any sense you ever had, you left in Jamaica. When I came back from the first World War, I had a crazy idea about developing a team spirit. But I learned the hard way that employees are like children. They don't want to think. They want to be told what to do and get paid for doing it."

Sally said, "Mr. Wynmill, this sounds very exciting."

Jonathan looked at her with a twinkle in his eye. "Mabel," he said, "I do have a first name. With our new open communication policy, it would save time if you just called me Jonathan."

At that moment, he was startled by groans coming from the portraits. There was a stabbing pain in his stomach. He felt sick. Very abruptly, he ended the meeting.

"I think we've covered enough for one day," he said gruffly. "I want you to meet me here at ten o'clock tomorrow morning. Please be on time."

When they left, he closed the door and slumped heavily into his chair. A chill enveloped his body. He was sweating profusely. "What have I done?" he moaned. "What an inane thing!"

In unison, the three portraits muttered, "You are trying to destroy everything we have held sacred." Then in a Grecian chant, "Shame, shame, shame."

That night was sleepless for Jonathan Wynmill. Early the next morning, he took a cold shower and returned to his office. At 9:30 AM he marched into the boardroom. At 9:59 his apprehension about the meeting was broken by a sound very foreign at Wynmill Industries. It was the laughter of the four vice presidents as they walked up the hall.

They were still chuckling when they entered the boardroom. Stanley explained that Sally had just told them a funny thing that happened to her in the parking lot. Sally shared the story with Jonathan.

The laughter died down, and Jonathan opened the meeting by asking for their thoughts on the proposed open communication policy.

At first, the vice presidents were reserved. But as the morning progressed, the conversation became very lively. Suggestions and innovative ideas flowed. Before they knew it, it was noon.

They agreed to break and continue the planning session the following morning. The enthusiasm of the vice presidents continued as they walked back to their offices.

While waiting for the elevator, Mabel said, "It's hard to believe the change that's come over Mr. Wynmill."

With a smile, Sally corrected her, "Don't you mean 'Jonathan'?"

Mabel said it might take a while for her to get used to that.

Then Ben asked, "Did you notice something different about the boardroom?"

"Yes," Mabel replied. "But I didn't think I should ask about it."

"Strange," Stanley said. "Why were the three portraits facing the wall?"

Moral:
Tradition is like ballast—too much can sink the ship.

28 Tale of Wall Street

Edgar Pope frantically looked for a payphone. When he found one at the corner of Broadway and Maiden Lane, he hurriedly made his call. "Betty," he said. "I'm in a rush, so listen carefully. I've got an interview that's going to make us rich! Draw out all our savings, and tonight we'll know how to invest and make a mint."

Fifteen minutes later, Edgar tried to compose himself as he sat in the waiting room of America's most recognized house of finance, Dow Jones, where the fiscal heartbeat of America has been monitored for generations. On the wall were graphs with peaks and valleys; one was titled "October 1929"; another was "October 1987"; and a third was "5,000 or Bust."

The receptionist was a tense woman whose expression changed frequently. With timing as consistent as a delayed windshield wiper, she alternated from a twitching smile to a worried look. The buzzer sounded. She picked up the telephone, listened intently and hung up.

"They'll see you now," she said, ushering Edgar into the inner sanctum. She introduced him to a short, balding man with a jolly face. "Mr. Dow," she said, "this is Edgar Pope, the newspaper reporter. As you may recall, you agreed to give him an interview."

"I did?" asked Mr. Dow. The receptionist frowned. "Ah, yes," Mr. Dow whispered, rolling his eyes. "I remember clearly." He gave Edgar a double handshake. "You're the young man who wants to learn all about the stock market."

"That's right," Edgar replied. "And I thought I'd be most fortunate if I could start with the two most knowledgeable people in this field."

"Ms. Jones, did you hear that?" Mr. Dow called across the room to a large woman with a mass of gray hair. She was smoking a pipe and reading an adult comic book, *How the Bull Chased the Bear into His Cave*.

"Now, Ms. Jones, put down your research," Mr. Dow insisted. "Our guest has just paid us a splendid compliment."

While Ms. Jones slowly made her way to join them, Edgar studied the large room. It was furnished with two antique desks facing one another. On the coffee table was a large crystal ball and a Ouija board. Beneath a five-foot Zodiac chart was a bookcase with volumes on astrology. From behind a draped wall came strange clicking and whirring noises, like finches in a bamboo thicket.

When they were seated together, Mr. Dow

picked up the conversation.

"One of the things you are going to enjoy about financial reporting is the fact that the stock market is very easy both to understand and to predict. Don't you agree, Ms. Jones?" She nodded. "First, you must understand that there are a thousand and one things that can affect the performance of the market."

He pressed a button on his desk. With a swish, the drapes opened, displaying a wall filled with hundreds of flashing panels.

Edgar got up to have a closer look. "I see each panel has a different title," he said.

"Right, Ms. Jones agreed. "All the things that determine the behavior of the stock market are listed alphabetically from right to left, bottom to top."

"As a starter," Mr. Dow explained, "you must learn the correct terminology for reporting the ups and downs of the market. For example, with a change of only five points, you should say that the market *inched, edged, slipped, pushed,* or *dipped.*" Edgar rapidly took notes. "A five- to fifteen-point change should be described as a *move, gain, lift, fall,* or *muted rebound.*"

Raising his hand, Edgar asked him to repeat as he checked his notes.

"And for your jumbo days," Mr. Dow went on, "use terms such as *fall, tumble, dive, soar, advance, sweep,* and *surge.*"

Ms. Jones spoke up as she relit her pipe. "Don't forget how to be evasive. My favorite line is: 'The market climbed higher on weak knees.'"

"I like that," Edgar commented.

"Now," Mr. Dow said, clasping his hands, "you're ready to learn how, with complete accuracy, to predict the behavior of the stock market. With this privileged information, you could end up a very wealthy fellow."

"Great!" exclaimed the reporter.

"Here are a few things that will always depress the market: rising inflation, moderate sales, profit-taking, falling interest rates, decline in the Tokyo market, and a strong dollar."

Edgar scribbled like a student cribbing for an exam.

Mr. Dow explained that positive influences on the market are large trading volumes, optimism about an upcoming summit meeting, no general upward pressure on industrial prices, reduction in corporate debt, and favorable interest rates for long-term Treasury bonds.

"Got it!" Edgar said, quickly turning to a new page of his note pad.

"I don't want to differ with my esteemed colleague," Ms. Jones said slowly. "But sometimes a strong dollar that has the negative effect of slowing exports can have a very positive effect in providing a rally for blue chip stocks."

"Not very likely," snapped Mr. Dow.

"It's *very* likely," disagreed Ms. Jones. "It happens time and again."

The atmosphere in the room became chilled. The three sat in silence, listening to the noises from the automated panels.

With a forced smile, Mr. Dow said to the reporter, "Of course, no one is infallible. We are not God."

"Speak for yourself," muttered Ms. Jones, puffing her pipe in high dudgeon. Turning to the reporter, she said, "To clarify the predictable actions of the market, you must realize that a more robust economy can spurt corporate earnings. But the higher interest rates that usually accompany rising inflation will increase the cost of doing business. And if the Federal Reserve cracks down and pushes short-term rates sharply higher to curb inflation, the economy could slip into a recession."

"That kind of reasoning confuses even me," said Mr. Dow.

"That's not hard to do," Ms. Jones replied.

"And furthermore," Mr. Dow shot back, "I still maintain that a strong dollar will depress the market."

"In a pig's eye," muttered Ms. Jones.

Mr. Dow's face turned red. "With my theory of market performance, I can recommend to this young man a stock portfolio that will enable him to retire in ten years."

"To sell apples!" added Ms. Jones. Without waiting for a reaction, she went on. "On the other hand, I can suggest a conservative number of stocks that will give him both security and potential for long-range growth."

Mr. Dow sniggered. "Like you did for your dentist. You're lucky he didn't sue you."

The crescendo of the argument increased. Edgar gathered his papers and tiptoed out of the room. Mr. Dow and Ms. Jones didn't even notice his leaving.

Out on the street, Edgar made another phone call. When he got an answer, he said, "Betty, I'm glad I caught you. About the savings account, don't do anything. I'll explain later."

Moral:
One who predicts with certainty is also an expert at reading tea leaves.

29 Salary Adjustment, at Your Own Expense

"Kid, you got a lot to learn," Albert Benson began. "And, my boy, what I'm going to teach you I bet you never learned in college."

Seated behind his battered desk, Benson thumped his fingers on the side of his big coffee mug. "The problem," he said, "is where to begin."

Dan, a new employee, sat on the edge of his chair.

Eying the young man critically, Benson said, "Since I'm moving up, I expect you'll be taking over a lot of my work. Believe me, it's going to take you a lot of time to learn about all the products we handle." He motioned to a bookcase filled with thick reference catalogues. "You got to be familiar with all this stuff."

"Wow, Mr. Benson!" Dan exclaimed, "that's a lot to learn."

"You bet." Stretching in his chair, Benson suggested that since he would have just one day with Dan, it would be a good idea to meet some of the customers. Benson handed him several legal-sized pads. "You better take these along, kid, in case you want to make notes."

"One will be enough," Dan said.

"Don't be silly. You can use them at home to jot down any business thoughts you might have." He reached into his bottom drawer and gave Dan a handful of handsome dark pens with the company logo. "You might just as well take these along, too."

As soon as they had driven out of the grounds, the on-the-job training began. Benson asked him, "How much do you think you're worth?"

Dan was not prepared for this question. He stumbled for an answer. "I don't know," he confessed. "I'm probably not worth much until I get some experience and can prove myself."

"That's the wrong answer," Benson said. "First thing you got to do is change your attitude. For example, when you get to be my age, you want to be successful like me, right?" Dan nodded. "Well, if you don't think you're worth more than you're being paid, nobody else will either. And you'll never amount to anything."

Dan said he never thought of it that way before.

"There's lots more things they don't teach you in college," Benson said, "mostly because they don't know it themselves." The young man politely agreed. "For example," Benson continued, "let's say you think you're worth fifteen percent more than you're being paid. What do you do about it?"

"I guess I just work hard until I get a salary

increase."

Benson shook his head. "Well, yes and no. Sure, you want that raise, but the system is set up so you don't have to wait. You'd never find that in a textbook, but the unwritten law in business is that you've got to take care of yourself."

As they sped along, Benson would take his eyes off the road and look at Dan to be sure he was paying attention. The young man kept checking his seat belt.

"Surviving is an art," Benson said. "You're not a machine that can only go this way and that way." He demonstrated by raising his right arm up and down like a piston. "No, sir," he continued. "You're a human being! And in this jungle you got lots of ways to take care of yourself."

"I guess you're right about that."

"So, to earn in advance what you're really worth, you first got to be convinced you deserve it. Then you learn to use the system. Never forget that the company you're working for has lots more money than you have. And they build into their budget a factor that enables you to adjust your income to what you think you're actually worth."

"Really?"

"Sure as spitting," Benson replied. "One easy way of developing a self-compensating plan is to start using the company phone for your personal long-distance calls. And definitely stick your own letters into the office postage machine."

Sensing that his mouth had opened, Dan closed it.

Benson dished out more advice. "Don't ever spend money paying to get copies made when you can do it at the office for nothing. And don't overlook the fringe benefit of time. If you sneak off to play golf or go to a movie on company time, that means you don't have to spend your own time doing this after work. So it's like a paid mini-vacation you can chalk up towards your salary adjustment."

Dan admitted this was a new concept for him.

"Sure it is," Benson agreed. "And I've just begun to teach you how to earn what you're really worth. Say that at the end of the month you haven't been able to adjust your net income to what you know it should be, that's when the expense account comes in handy."

By that time they had arrived at their first stop, and the lesson was suspended. After the client visit, Benson decided it was time for lunch. A few miles down the road, he pulled into a restaurant parking lot.

Seated at a table near the window, he ordered clams on the half shell, oyster stew, Caesar salad, and a sirloin steak, medium well. When Dan ordered a cup of soup and a tuna fish sandwich, Benson waited until the waitress walked away before admonishing him.

"My boy," he said, "when the company is paying, this has got to be your main meal of the day."

When they finished, Benson noticed the bill was unusually low because of Dan's sandwich. He then told the waitress to box up one of the coconut cakes in the display counter and add it to the bill. He winked at Dan and said, "Just as well have a nice surprise when I get home tonight."

Back in the car, Benson resumed his lecture. "As I told you, save your expense account to make up any deficit in your self-compensation plan. Like today, we might have had a customer with us. So I could easily adjust the cost item for the lunch. I read that over a five-year period, the president of Lone Star Cement let the company pay for over a million dollars of his personal expenses. Now that's a prime example of salary adjustment!"

"It sure is."

"Another company I wished I worked for is Digital Equipment."

"Why's that?"

"I read that in one year their expense accounts were stretched $30 million. Why, one of their people spent over a thousand bucks on a bar bill. Another blew three grand for a dinner cruise. And there was a fat limousine charge."

"You sure know the angles," Dan said.

"Aw, it's nothing," Benson said modestly. "I know I shouldn't have given you the whole bale of hay at one time, but I've only got this one day with you."

"Won't I be seeing you in your new position?"

"Nope. I'm moving into top management, but not at this company. The bastards gave me my notice last week. I haven't decided yet where I'm going to go. Maybe I'll take it easy for a while. Since I put my trip to Florida on my sick leave, the company will have to pay for two weeks' vacation plus three weeks' severance. So, you can see, I'm coming out smelling like roses."

Dan told him he was sorry they wouldn't be working together.

"Don't worry, kid," Benson said. "Just remember what I taught you, and you got it made."

Moral:
***As the expense account is bent,
so goes the company.***

30 Paul's Tale

As he waited in the lobby of the country club, Paul had mixed feelings about the evening. He was looking forward to seeing Jerry Goodman, his ex-employer, who recently returned from a year-long trip around the world. He considered Jerry to be one of his closest friends. Yet he agonized over the questions he knew he would be asked.

Paul remembered how happy Jerry was when he began his vacation. "For the first time in my life," Jerry said, "I'm going to forget about Goodman Paper Company. You heard me tell our new president the ball's in his court."

Now, as Jerry approached him, Paul noticed a haggard expression on his suntanned face. There were dark circles beneath his eyes; his walk was that of a much older man.

Jerry exclaimed. "It's great to see you again. Come on, let's have a drink before dinner." After they sat down in the lounge, Jerry began reminiscing.

"Paul," he said, "you look as young as you did

ten years ago when I hired you as vice president of Human Resources."

Jerry gave the drink order and stretched as he sat back. "God," he moaned, "what a fool I've been. I can't believe a 65-year-old man could have been so stupid. Hell, I thought our new president hung the moon. But he's damned near ruined my business!"

When Jerry had first said he wanted to relinquish more control so that he could travel, Paul suggested he find someone else to be president. Jerry offered him the job, and he refused. Instead, Paul recommended using an executive search firm to find suitable candidates.

The third person Jerry interviewed was Calvin Hardman, who came with high endorsements. For a man in his early thirties, he had an impressive background: Ivy League universities, executive positions in three major corporations, and several published articles. He explained he left each previous job because his superiors failed to appreciate his talents.

At the time Jerry was impressed. He said to Paul, "You know, I hardly got out of high school. Never went to college. When I look at this guy's resume, I'm astounded. He's got an M.B.A. and more degrees than I have golf clubs. With his fancy clothes and Boston accent, he makes me feel like a nerd."

Paul was skeptical and cautioned Jerry not to act too fast. Giving up the reins was not easy for Jerry. Finally, in a resigned tone, he said to Paul, "In business you've got to accept change. This Hardman fellow—he's as different from me as night is to day. But, he's probably a lot smarter. I'm going to hire him because I do want to get away."

At first, the new president flattered Jerry profusely and treated department heads as if they were brilliant siblings. Hardman especially complimented Paul, stressing the value of good employee relations.

Pleased with Calvin Hardman's performance, Jerry left for his twelve-month trip. In the following weeks, Paul hoped he was wrong in thinking that the new president had a sudden change in attitude. It appeared that his arrogance increased in proportion to Jerry's distance from home.

It was something new for the door to the president's office to be kept closed. To see the top executive, the managers had to make an appointment. After each meeting, the president insisted that employees submit their thoughts in writing—just for the record.

The first time Calvin Hardman asked Paul to join him for a cup of coffee, he announced that he was demanding more formality within the organization. He ordered Paul to refer to him as "Mr. Hardman." His final comment was, "And I expect you to see to it that the employees treat me with proper respect."

To keep employees on their toes, the new president toured the plant once a week. He called this his "observing tour." If he found employees talking to one another, he would sneak up behind them, let out a startling "So!" and walk away. Occasionally, at noon he stuck his head inside the lunchroom. He would stare around the room, shout "Ah ha!", then close the door.

Paul was inundated with employees asking what was going on. He tried to convince them that Mr. Hardman's behavior was typical of one who has just assumed the top role in a corporation. With his fingers crossed behind his back, he assured them that this erratic behavior, like chicken pox, would soon disappear.

Paul's second summons to the executive suite began with Mr. Hardman announcing he had uncovered a serious breach in personnel practices. By studying the time sheets, he had discovered "favoritism" towards an employee named Joey Tomkins.

Paul told him that Joey was a yard hand who been with the company for many years. He had suffered a heart attack. When he returned to work, he wasn't up to heavy manual labor, so Jerry found him an office job.

"But what about this overtime?" the president asked like an interrogator.

Paul explained that since Joey was now making less money per hour, he let him work overtime. "Also," he added, "this saved us the expense of hiring another person, who we needed."

"This is against my policy," Mr. Hardman said. "But you are vice president for these matters. It's your decision." He paused for a moment, then said in a deep voice, "Practice your welfare elsewhere, not at the expense of this company. We can't afford both you and this Joey person. So you decide which of you is going to stay."

Paul slowly rose from his seat. "Yes," he said quietly, "I'll let you know." He returned to his office, and wrote his resignation.

When Paul told the story to his wife, Doris, she boiled, "Get in touch with Jerry Goodman," she cried.

"I don't know where he is," he answered.

It was the first time since he was twelve that Paul had been unemployed. The rest of that week seemed like a series of endless Sundays. Doris assured him he had done the right thing. "Now," she said optimistically, "let's work together on a new resume. Then you can start looking for that ideal job that's waiting for you somewhere out there."

News travels fast in a small community. Word of Paul's situation spread like wildfire, because Doris spent most of the next day on the telephone. Several mill employees came to say they were planning to support Paul with a protest. He talked them out of it.

The following Monday, Paul received a call from the Westman Photo Company. Having heard of Paul's resignation, the chief operations officer invited him to meet that afternoon. Paul was offered the job of vice president for community relations. He quickly accepted.

But Paul couldn't help thinking about the problems Jerry would find when he returned.

Now back at the club, instead of quizzing Paul about happenings at the plant, Jerry said, "Incidentally, I have the full story about what that bastard did to you. But don't worry, I fired him this morning."

Jerry looked Paul in the eye and said, hesitatingly, "Because of your loyalty to the Westman Company, I doubt that you would leave. But if you want it, the president's job is your's." For a second time, Paul turned down this offer.

Mr. Hardman was not heard from again. Then one day Jerry received a computerized mailing from an outfit called Creative Business and Commerce, Ltd. It was selling a six-cassette course covering these subjects: How to motivate your employees; change failure to success; develop new growth; cultivate additional clients; structure an effective team; outpace your competitors.

At the bottom of the advertisement, Jerry read "written and narrated by Calvin Hardman."

Moral:
Give the keys to your clone, not a clown.

31 Yellow Butterfly and Pigeon with Pink Toes

The transformation of Joseph "Bull" Silver at age fifty-three was triggered by a statement from a five-year-old. This saying had more effect on his life than had a whole year of therapy. His about-face in behavior even changed his relationship with Mrs. Van der Hoffen, who had previously defined him as "my nemesis *numero uno.*"

Prior to this amazing transition, his nickname well described him. His dominant character was first seen by his kindergarten teacher. She found that when she left the classroom, she would return to find all the toys in the room piled on top of his desk.

After college, Bull borrowed the downpayment on a back-hoe digging machine. One success followed another. Twenty-five years later, the Joseph Silver Excavating Company was the largest road builder and earthmover in the state.

With his community work, Bull displayed the same drive that made him a successful businessman. It was through his charity work that he saw the inside of many elaborate homes where he would never have been invited socially. It was during one of these occasions that he made a decision which caused repercussions among the city's most prominent socialites.

At Mrs. Van der Hoffen's mansion in the exclusive Primark neighborhood, Bull attended a planning meeting for the upcoming Children's Relief Fund Ball. As he was leaving, he commented that he would like to build a home in the neighborhood. Mrs. Van der Hoffen tersely informed him that no lots were available.

Later, however, Bull purchased the Brownleigh house across the street from Mrs. Van der Hoffen. He demolished the building, and over the next two years constructed a four-story marble edifice. He instructed a renowned Chicago architect to model it after a Venetian palazzo he had seen in *National Geographic*.

This turn of events led Mrs. Van der Hoffen to insomnia. To everyone from her most intimate friends to the postman, she bemoaned what was happening to the Primark neighborhood. As Bull's home neared completion, she developed migraine headaches. Her wise doctor recommended six months in Europe. She took his advice and moved to the continent with her maid, chauffeur, and two white toy poodles.

Unfortunately, two days after Mrs. Van der Hoffen returned, the Silver home was opened to the public as a fund-raiser for the Children's Relief Fund. As president of the organization, she felt

"My new neighbor has placed in his front yard a ten-foot statue of a man selling balloons. Oh, mon Dieu!" cried Mrs. Van der Hoffen.

---

obligated to attend.

The next day, during tea with a friend, Mrs. Van der Hoffen described the event. "The interior of the house," she said, "is as cozy as a wing of the Metropolitan Museum. I assure you that Mr. Silver's only taste is in his mouth. *Ah, le parvenu.*" Her friend made a few commiserating remarks. "In addition, my new neighbor has placed in the front yard a ten-foot statue of a man selling balloons. I hear he paid fifty thousand dollars to a leading French sculptor. *Oh, mon Dieu!*"

Several years later, Bull took his little granddaughter to the zoo. That night, his wife, Rose, was puzzled by his different manner.

Holding a daisy from the flowered centerpiece, he said, "Did you notice the color of this blossom? Just look at the perfect design of the petals."

She gave a surprised laugh. "Bull? You? A philosopher?"

"You know," he said earnestly, "maybe I've spent my life barking up a tree for something I already have right in front of my nose."

Rose became concerned. She asked if he was having any business problems. Suspecting bad news from his recent physical examination, she quizzed him about his health. "Don't try to kid me," she said. "You're holding something back."

He smiled and assured her that everything was fine. Later, when they were in bed, his last comment before turning out the light was, "To appreciate the beauty in the small things all around you, all you've got to do is open your eyes."

Rose kept her eyes open for over an hour. In the dark beside her, Bull slept like a child. Finally, with a deep and disturbed sigh, she fell asleep.

The following morning, the next person to notice the change was Bull's assistant. She was struck by his calm, modulated voice. He commented that he liked her blue dress, and asked about her daughter who had just entered college. Prior to that moment, she was not aware he even knew she had a family.

That afternoon, on his routine site inspections, Bull's placid approach amazed his employees. At the end of the day, as he was leaving his last location, his manager asked, "Bull, are you feeling O.K.?"

He smiled and replied, "Yes, I've never felt better. But you know something funny? You're the sixth person today who's asked that."

From that day on, the image of the old, strident Bull faded. His booming voice and frenetic behavior disappeared, while the reserved and considerate manner of his new personality provided energy and direction.

One summer evening, Bull saw Mrs. Van der Hoffen taking her neighborhood stroll. He called to her, then crossed the street. Pointing to the statue of the balloon man, he said, "I would like to get your opinion. I'm thinking about changing that statue for something more in keeping with our neighborhood, like a tree that flowers this time of the year. I'd appreciate your advice."

Surprised, she agreed to give this thought.

"I want to donate the balloon man to the Children's Relief Fund," Bull said. "Because of the good work you've done, I want to put a plaque on the base of the statue to honor you."

This was an historic moment. It was the only time in the memory of those residing in the Primark community that Mrs. Van der Hoffen was without words.

A few weeks later, Bull was having a drink in his

library while his wife opened the mail. Suddenly she let out a gasp. "Look at this!" she exclaimed. "An invitation to dinner at Mrs. Van der Hoffen's."

"What's the occasion?" he asked.

"It's a handwritten note inviting us to a small gathering of her special friends."

Bull took a long sip of his drink. "Well, what do you know," he smiled.

That night, before falling asleep, Bull turned to his wife. She was propped up in bed, working a crossword puzzle. "The most important things in life are those little things," he said wistfully.

"If you say so," Rose replied, as she filled in a word.

"Yes," he said. "Life really has meaning when you accept beauty in the ordinary."

"Mmmm," she responded, biting the end of her pencil.

"For example," Bull continued, "you remember last summer when I took little Emma to the zoo? I made sure she saw the elephants, the hippopotamus, the giant pandas—even a giraffe nibbling the top of a tree. Driving home, I asked her which animal she liked the most. Guess what she said."

Rose put down her crossword puzzle. "I'll say the elephants."

"Nup," Bull said. "It was a yellow butterfly and the pigeon with pink toes."

Moral:

Let your lasting monument be invisible.